JAYDEN THOMPSON

DIAMOND
IN THE
ROUGH

Second edition
ISBN: 979-8-9924339-0-6

To all the authors who inspired me to write.
Thank you.

DIAMOND IN THE ROUGH

ONE

My 21st birthday would be the day I died, and unfortunately for me, that day came tomorrow.

The prison was quiet enough to hear a pin drop, the deadly kind of silence that was enough to set me on edge. My breathing was the only sound. I sprawled across the single cot, staring up at the cracks in the ceiling. My legs dangled over the edge because this cot wasn't made for someone of my size. Nothing in this prison was. Even the orange jumpsuit was too tight in the arms and a few inches too short in the legs. Some items were hard to come by in the wastelands, and nobody was willing to risk their life fighting through mutants to make sure an inmate was dressed properly.

For whatever reason, I found myself wishing for a clock. There were no windows or clocks or anything in this building to judge the time by. I only had the word of the guards, but most of them went out of their way to ignore me. Luke told me this morning it was the day before my birthday, but I had no way of knowing when the transition from *today* to *tomorrow* would come. The wait would kill me long before the syringe of poison in the hospital tomorrow would.

This cell had been my home for six months now. Six months of waiting. Six months of wondering if Slater would come through on his promise—and six months of disappointment as he ignored me and left me to rot.

I'd been here long enough that I knew every crack and crevice of this cell. I knew exactly how many tiles were on the ceiling and how many bars were on the door. I knew the name, rank, and approximate age of every guard that came through here. I had created a daily exercise routine consisting of push-ups and squats and lunges and anything I could do using just my bodyweight. I had read every book in the pitiful prison library a dozen times—they were all old books about the pre-Virus government—and had played so many games of solitaire with the battered deck of cards sitting on the end of the bed that I was sure at some point I had become a world-renowned expert at it.

For six months, I had entertained myself the best that one stuck in a prison cell could. But now, when I could really use something to keep my mind off my situation, I was fresh out of ideas.

My gaze snagged on the deck of cards I'd tossed to the end of the bed. I sighed as I slid the cards out of the dented, battered box and settled into the familiar motions of shuffling the deck and laying the cards out on the floor. It didn't fully take my mind off of what happened at ten o'clock tomorrow, but it helped.

I made it through four entire games before the dull stomp of boots interrupted the silence of the prison. I froze. There was only one prisoner in this building, only one person they could be here to see.

No. It couldn't be time already—I'd taken a nap earlier to pass the time, but I hadn't slept *that* long, had I?

My fingers shook as I gathered up the cards to slide them back into their box, not giving the newcomers the satisfaction of looking up, even as the footsteps came to a halt right out-side of my cell. Judging by the sound, there were at least three of them. They let a few beats of silence pass before one of them spoke.

"Good afternoon, Ethan."

The crisp voice had me shooting to my feet, cards scattering everywhere.

President Slater stood on the other side of the bars, his gray eyes narrowed on me. He wore his military uniform, his medals gleaming, the gray streaks in his dark hair especially pronounced under the harsh white light. His eyes were the color of steel, sharp enough to cut a person in half when he wielded them right.

This was the man who had once been a father to me. This was the man who let me down when I needed him.

My jaw clenched. "Mr. President."

His eyes narrowed further as he noted the tension in my shoulders. A guard flanked him on either side, their hands within easy reach of the guns holstered at their sides. Slater jerked his chin at them and said, "Leave us."

The one on the left started. "But sir, he's a killer."

"And he's behind bars," Slater said dismissively, even as the word stung me to the core. "Go."

They exchanged a look but obediently filed out. Slater turned back to me to find that I was glaring at him with every ounce of anger I had. Slater was a man of authority. He was a man of power.

But right now, he just looked exhausted.

"There's no need for that," he said softly.

"No need for what?" I snapped. "I'm supposed to be executed tomorrow!"

"Ethan—"

"Save it," I snarled. "Where the hell have you been? You promised you would get me a pardon, but you left me to rot away in a prison cell for six months instead!" My fingers curled around the metal bars that served as the only barrier between Slater and I. His guards had reason to worry. I'd punch Slater in the face if I wasn't locked up. It was taking everything I had to resist the urge to reach through the bars and grab him by the throat. "One of your men betrayed me, and you did *nothing*."

Slater dragged a hand through his hair. "Damn it, Ethan, don't you think I tried? Pardons have to go through the Council, but they didn't approve of yours."

I squeezed the bars so tight my knuckles turned white. "You should have made them."

"How? They're stubborn as bulls. I've been trying for six months."

"Have you? It seems to me that if you were really trying, you would have at least come to tell me about it." My breathing turned ragged. "How many requests have I put in to see you? How many times have you ignored them? Ignored *me?*"

He met my gaze evenly. "The public is unaware that you worked for me. The Council requested we keep it that way, so I kept my distance to avoid any unwanted rumors."

"The *public*," I snarled, "has labeled me as a *serial killer.*"

The words rang through the halls. Slater flinched. "You knew the risks—"

"Of course I knew the risks. But I also knew that you would keep your promise and get me the damn pardon. The whole reason I pleaded guilty is because I just *knew* you would come through for me. But not only do you not uphold your promise, you ignore me the entire time." I looked down, my anger evaporating. "Did you know a councilman came in here yesterday? He wanted to inform me of the *details of my execution.*"

The Council didn't approve of putting anyone under

twenty-one years of age on Death Row. They arrested me when I was twenty. My birthday was tomorrow. They would take me to the hospital at ten o'clock in the morning to inject poison into my neck. I wouldn't live long enough to remember what happened next.

A lethal syringe. Quick, painless, and efficient. Slater's preferred method of death.

"That is what I came here to talk about," Slater said quietly.

I let out a humorless laugh and stepped away from the bars. "It's a little too late for that."

"Is it?"

I paused at his tone. "What do you mean?"

He leaned against the bars, his voice dropping so it sounded conspiratorial. "The Council has been trying to get my approval for an infrastructure project for a year now. They brought it up again in our meeting this morning, and I used it to my advantage to work a deal. I convinced them it was a waste to kill off such talent at such a young age, and that if they gave you a reprieve, I would agree to the project. They accepted the deal."

I wasn't quite sure that I was breathing. He'd done it. There was no time to spare, but he'd done it. He'd refused to talk to me for six months, and I'd used the time to blame him for my predicament, but it seemed that he finally came through.

"You got my pardon?" I breathed.

He winced. "No, not quite. But I got you out of execution."

I blinked, my hope vanishing. "What does that mean?"

"Both the Council and I had to compromise in order to get what we wanted. They don't want the public finding out about your involvement with the government, so they are unwilling to let you walk free. I cut a deal, Ethan. I must warn you that it isn't desirable, but it is better than what you have now."

I would take *not desirable* over *dead* any day of the week. "What is it?"

Slater squared his shoulders, his tired gray eyes meeting mine, his expression grim. "Exile."

T W O

"Exile?" I echoed, my voice hoarse.

Slater's jaw clenched. "It's the best I can do, Ethan. The Council doesn't want the public knowing that you worked for me."

"But I did."

He sighed, raking a hand through his hair. "I know."

I scoffed as I stepped back, lacing my fingers behind my head in an effort to dispel the tension running through every nerve. Exile meant being thrown outside of the city's impenetrable walls and never being let back in. It meant being barred from every Safe Zone in America. It meant spending the night out in the wastelands among the crumbling buildings and hazardous conditions.

It meant being out *there*, where the mutants roamed.

But it also meant I got to live—because living with the mutants would be better than the syringe that awaited me tomorrow.

"I can't believe this," I muttered. "You're exiling me for doing what *you* told me to do."

"Yes," Slater hissed, "because I thought you'd rather live in the wastelands than a coffin six feet under. The Council wants you *dead*. This is the best you are going to get." He sighed again. "For now, anyway."

My eyes narrowed. "What does that mean?"

"I'm trying everything in my power to get the Council to change their decision. If I give it some time, I'm sure I'll be able to convince them—"

"You've had six months to convince them." I sat down on the bed, kicking my long legs up as I glared at Slater. "I don't see what you can say now that will change their minds."

The corner of his lips curled into a half-hearted smile. "I guess I deserve that."

I crossed my arms.

Slater angled his head, the light catching the streaks of silver in his hair. "Do you want to be executed or would you like to try your hand at exile?"

My teeth ground together. What choice did I have? "Exile."

"That's what I thought." He leaned against the bars. "Tomorrow at ten o'clock. You'll be given a bag of supplies and escorted to the gate. There's a hundred rules that somebody will tell you, but the most important is you can't come within three hundred yards of any Safe Zone wall or any official transportation running between the Zones. Breaching these restrictions or attacking any civilian or government official will result in teams going out to put you down like a rabid dog."

I swallowed. "Got it."

"Mingling with other exiles or roamers isn't banned," Slater continued, "but I encourage you to be careful in that regard." He didn't have to tell me that; I already knew that the roamers, who punished themselves with self-exile, had a tendency to be insane. "Likewise, killing such people, whether in self-defense or otherwise, is allowed. What you do with yourself in exile is up to you, as long as it doesn't interfere with government business or put any civilians in harm's way. Do you understand?"

"Yes."

Slater nodded. "I believe in you, Ethan. I've known you for a long time, and I know you won't have any trouble surviving out there. Think of it as another mission. It'll be rough, yes, but not impossible. If I thought you couldn't handle it, I wouldn't have presented this as an option."

I arched a brow. "Am I supposed to thank you?"

His steely eyes met mine. "All I ask is that you stay safe out there."

I looked down. "No promises."

He stepped away from the door with practiced elegance, leaving the space between us empty and cold. A shiver worked its way down my spine as I held Slater's piercing gray gaze. He paused for a moment, staring back at me as if he had something else to say, but then he turned away with a slight shake of his head. I watched him walk down the hallway, his steps neat and controlled, all the way to the door at the end, where his guards greeted him with suspicious glances in my direction.

I leaned my head against the wall behind me. *Exile.* It was better than execution; I wasn't doubting that. But I wanted a pardon. Slater had always assured me that if my position were compromised, he would bail me out.

He *promised.*

I knew that Slater and the Council didn't always see eye-to-eye, but I thought he had a little more sway over them than he claimed.

And now I was being exiled.

My parents died in the wastelands when I was eight, ripped apart by mutants while on a supply run. We never got along; they viewed me as nothing but an extra mouth to feed. I barely batted an eye when I was told what happened to them. It was freeing in a twisted sort of way.

Slater was the vice president at the time. He had known my father and came to comfort me, but I'd shocked him by not being upset. He took this for strength rather than indifference and decided to take me under his wing. The post-Virus government was very different from the one I read about that lived before the Virus. This government had no problem in taking a child and forging him into a weapon. Slater himself trained me until the president died and he took his place. Another thing about the post-Virus government—presidential elections were nonexistent. There was a president, and if he became unfit to serve, the vice president took his place until he, too, died or became unfit.

When Slater became leader, he decided it was time to put me on the field. Though no one came out and said it explicitly, I was his assassin. I did my job efficiently and without question. I took out rebel leaders and bands of exiles and political opponents—anyone who threw a wrench in the government's plans as they tried to smooth out the destruction caused by the Virus. I never hated it, though I never enjoyed it, either. It was my job. It was what I was trained to do. My position got me special training and extra ration points and anything I needed. Most people weren't so lucky and I knew better than to complain.

But things changed six months ago, when Slater assigned me with another agent to take out a group of rebels stirring up trouble in the north. The other agent and I never got along. We hated each other, in fact, and all it took was one disagreement for him to sell me out to the people we were supposed to kill. I made it out, only to be arrested upon returning to Austin. The media ate it up, the phrase *Ethan Ellis: Serial Killer* blaring across every news channel in the remnants of the country. There wasn't enough information to prove I had been working for the government, not when I'd been sworn to secrecy and cleared my tracks, so the news labeled me as some glorified killer. I was charged with 37 counts of murder. I pleaded guilty at my trial, holding on to Slater's promise that he would pardon me, since I'd only been doing his work from the start.

But Slater hadn't come through, and here I was.

I squeezed my eyes shut and tried to sleep, something—*anything*—to make the time pass faster so I didn't have to dread what happened in the morning.

"Ethan!"

I jolted awake. It took me a minute to register that someone had awakened me, to realize that the same someone was now standing on the other side of the bars, his head cocked to the side as he watched me.

Luke's brow furrowed as he looked me over. "You look like shit, man."

I glared at him as I stumbled to my feet. I must have finally slipped into a deeper sleep, enough so that I didn't hear Luke coming—a rare occurrence, considering how loud the door down the hall was and how every footstep echoed off the hallway.

Luke had brown hair and eyes to match, his dark skin a stark contrast to Slater's pale complexion. A thick scar cut its way through his left eyebrow. He wore a simple black military uniform, a bulletproof vest over his chest and a rifle slung across his back. There was a tray of food in his hand. He slid it through the slot in the bottom of the door, the plastic tray scraping across the concrete floor.

I blinked at the meal. Toast and bacon and eggs. Breakfast food. Which meant—

I swore under my breath. "What time is it?"

"Just before midnight," Luke said, checking his watch. "Don't worry. It isn't morning yet."

My shoulders sagged in relief. As much as I hated this cell, as much as I wanted to get out and to see sunshine and feel fresh air again, I hadn't quite mentally prepared myself for exile yet. At least in prison, I didn't have to hunt for food or fight monsters to stay alive. It would take days to gather up enough supplies for me to feel even remotely safe out there. I eyed the rifle Luke carried. A weapon like that would sure come in handy.

Not that anyone here would allow me to have it. The other guards hadn't even trusted me with anything other than a plastic spoon to eat with.

Luke sat cross-legged on the floor and helped himself to a piece of bacon. "I heard Slater cut you a deal. They weren't planning on feeding you in the morning, so I thought you could use some nourishment before you go out into the wastelands."

I gave him a nod of thanks and sat down as well, mimicking Luke's position. Before I got arrested, I had known him in passing, but ever since I had been locked up, he made an effort to be friendly with me, sometimes going as far as playing a game of cards with me through the bars of the cell. I couldn't even bring myself to be angry with him for keeping me from escaping. He was a soldier doing his job.

After all, I had only been doing my job, and look where it landed me.

Luke licked his fingers. "So what's the plan once you get into the wastelands?"

I shrugged. "Survive."

"That's it? They say the roamers have more freedom than anybody. You could do anything you wanted to."

"The roamers are crazy, and I won't be leaving by choice. I'm being exiled." I folded a piece of toast in half and took a bite out of it. "Besides, I work better alone. Slater knows that."

"Slater screwed you over."

"Tell me something I don't already know," I said, rolling my eyes.

Luke fell silent, and the two of us made quick work of devouring the tray of food. When it was gone, I kicked the tray aside and spread out the deck of cards, dealing some to myself and to Luke.

He studied his cards with a slight frown. "What I meant about your plans," he said, laying down the first card, "is that I think you should probably hook up with one of the groups out there. Some of them are crazy, but you would stand to benefit with the right one."

"The roamers are crazy and the exiles are criminals. Best to stay away from both."

"Maybe." He flipped another card towards me. "But someone with your abilities could probably take them on without a problem."

He gave me a pointed look as he said this. I'd trained as an assassin for most of my life. Even without knowing that, my appearance alone was enough to intimidate most people, given I was taller than everyone I had ever met. I towered over everyone, Luke and Slater included.

"I'll already have the mutants to deal with," I said. "Having to sleep with one eye open because I'm afraid someone will kill me in my sleep is something I don't want to worry about."

He shrugged. "Then find someone that you trust."

"I don't trust anyone."

"That's your problem."

I narrowed my eyes. The wastelands were notoriously ruthless. It was a kill-or-be-killed kind of world outside the Safe Zones. I'd completed enough missions for Slater out there to know that putting my trust in one roamer was dangerous, much less an entire group of them. It just wasn't safe out there.

I selected a card from my hand and placed it on the pile to buy myself some time to think of a response.

"I can handle it," I said finally.

Luke angled his head. "Are you sure? I mean, I've seen the people who have been out there since the beginning. The original survivors. They are crazy as shit, man. Being out there in the wastelands on their own for that many years… It drives them to insanity."

Luke should know. His family had been out there from the beginning.

"They've been out there for thirty years," I said. "I haven't even started yet."

"If you plan on living a full life, then *you* will be out there for that long."

I picked at the corner of my card. "If I find myself in need of help, then I can look for it. But I'll cross that bridge when I get to it."

"*If* you get to it," Luke muttered ominously.

I glowered at him. "I'm having trouble deciding if you are rooting for me or not."

"Of course I'm rooting for you," he said. "Slater screwed you over, and if the president is willing to drag the guy he practically adopted through the mud, then that worries me about the future of the military. You aren't a bad guy, Ethan." He paused. "If we forget all the killing, that is."

"I was doing what I was told," I growled.

He held up his hands in surrender. "I know. That's why I'm rooting for you."

I held his gaze for a few long moments before letting my head drop. "Thanks."

"No problem," he said, dropping his last card onto the pile between us, nestled between the bars of the cell. "I win."

"Play again?"

"Why not?"

I shuffled the cards. Luke's words echoed through my head. He was right about me needing a plan, but working with the roamers or the other exiles? That was asking for a knife in the back. It was too dangerous.

My jaw clenched as I dealt a fresh hand of cards to both of us.

"Do you have any other wonderful words of wisdom to share with me?" I asked Luke.

He tilted his head, considering. "Don't die?"

"That seems like a given."

He shrugged. "I dunno. I think there's a rule about exiles not being able to come within so many feet of the Safe Zone walls—"

"Three hundred yards."

"Right. So don't do that."

I snorted. "You're a lot of help."

He lifted a scarred brow. "I daresay I'm more help to you than anyone else in this city."

I rolled my eyes. Luke flashed a crooked grin before swiping up his hand of cards. He took one look at them and swore colorfully.

We played another hand of cards and were starting on the third round when Luke's watch beeped. I went still as he checked it.

"Midnight," he said quietly. He glanced up at me. "Happy birthday, Ethan."

I was twenty-one years old.

Happy birthday, indeed.

THREE

My birthday proved to be a bleak day. I found myself thankful for the thick layer of clouds that blotted out the sky, not just because the dreary morning reflected my mood just fine, but because unfiltered sunlight after six months in a windowless prison cell wouldn't have been good on my eyes. The last thing I wanted was for the cameras to capture me squinting.

At precisely a quarter to ten, Luke and a few other guards appeared outside of my cell. They ordered me to change out of my prison jumpsuit into a simple gray t-shirt, jacket, and pants, and then marched me down the hall, my hands cuffed in front of me.

I expected to be led outside, but the one in charge—his name was Martin, and we had a mutual dislike of each other—took an unexpected left turn and led me into the infirmary.

My steps slowed. "What are we doing here?"

Martin nodded at the single nurse in the room, who picked up a large object that was vaguely shaped like a syringe.

I stopped entirely. "What is this?"

Slater said I wouldn't be executed. He said I was being exiled, not given a syringe.

Panic began to set in.

"Chill," Luke murmured. "It's a tracker. All exiles get one so we can keep track of your location."

Martin sneered at me. "It's so we know if any criminals get

too close to the walls."

Luke shrugged. "That too."

He gave me a reassuring nod, so I held out my cuffed arms. The nurse shoved my sleeve back and stuck the needle—the biggest needle I'd ever seen in my life—just below the crook of my elbow. I gritted my teeth at the stab of pain. She pushed down the plunger and I felt something sliding under my skin, traces of pain radiating from the source.

I didn't miss Martin's smirk over the nurse's shoulder.

She yanked the syringe out and tossed it on the table without ever meeting my gaze. Martin tapped at a computer on the other side of the room, no doubt checking if the tracker was working. Whatever he saw on it satisfied him, and he herded me out of the room with a final nod to the nurse.

This time, he led the way right through the front doors. I relished the cool breeze against my skin as I walked out of the prison, seeing the outside for the first time in half a year.

Slater and the entire Council waited by the main gate. The sky above was a perfect color to match Slater's eyes as he looked at me, his expression unreadable.

The massive wall that protected the city was a towering fortress behind them. They constructed the Safe Zones of America in the first few months after the Virus hit. Major cities built giant walls around themselves to keep their people safe. Austin, Texas was the first to complete its wall, and as a result, it became the new capital of the country. The cities let in everyone who could make it there, but soon faced a shortage of space and closed their doors, leaving the rest to fend for themselves. The areas between the Zones were now ruined and ravaged, full of mutants and a few rogue bands of roamers who had somehow managed to survive.

I stared up at the massive concrete-and-steel wall that now

surrounded Austin and realized I would soon be joining them.

One councilman's voice pulled me out of my thoughts. "Ethan Ellis, you are here today to face punishment for your crimes against the country." I turned and realized it was the same guy who had appeared in my cell the other day, the one who had informed me of the details of my execution. He was a short, balding man with hazel eyes that were narrowed on me. He didn't look happy to be out here; I had a feeling he'd been one to push for my death instead of exile. "By order of President Slater of the United States of America, you are sentenced to indefinite exile. Do you have any last requests?"

Slater cut in, "He earlier requested survival gear, which will be given to him once he's outside of the gate."

I hadn't asked for any such thing, but I sent a silent thank-you to Slater for thinking of it. For all my problems with him, I knew he would get me enough gear to help me survive the first few days. From there, I could get enough resources to make it on my own.

The councilman nodded and proceeded to rattle off a list of rules I was supposed to follow during exile. I didn't pay attention to most of it, only listening to the parts about how I would be killed if I came within three hundred yards of any Safe Zone wall or official military transport. I let my gaze trail across the city skyline, soaking it in. This was the last time I'd be able to step foot inside a Safe Zone again, the last time I would ever see my hometown. My gaze snagged on one building in particular—my apartment building. I could even see the narrow window that led to my room from here.

My hands curled into fists, sending a faint pain shooting up the arm the nurse had stabbed with the giant syringe.

The councilman finished his list of rules and looked around expectantly. The rest of the Council and the gathered crowd shuffled on their feet. It was a large crowd, I realized, a line of soldiers holding them back. Cameras flashed from all around. I stood my ground, feet shoulder-width apart and chin held high. The Council rarely made such a spectacle out of exile, which is why everyone looked so uncomfortable now, but I guessed the news coverage I'd been getting called for drastic measures.

I watched as Slater signaled to the guards at the top of the gate. He and the Council moved out of the way as the guards hit a button and the massive steel gates swung open. My own guards nudged me from behind, and I stepped forward, my throat constricting as I stared down the crumbled street beyond the gate. The skyline out there was much different from the one inside the walls. A snarl rumbled from somewhere out of sight, and the soldiers clutched their guns, expecting a mutant to come leaping out at any instant.

Gritting my teeth, I walked towards the gates, not giving myself any room to show weakness. Luke murmured a soft, "Good luck," as I passed, but I didn't look at him or anybody else.

A harsh wind swept by me as I stepped past the gates. The wall had buffered it, but now it hit me with full force. The gates swung shut behind me with a groan. I glanced back to see Slater's dark gaze pinned on me before he vanished behind a wall of concrete and steel.

A simple black backpack waited a few feet away. It looked like it had been tossed there indifferently, possibly breaking whatever was inside, but my eyes found the small key hanging from a ring on the side. On the opposite side hung a coil of thick rope, and the cup holders held water bottles. I walked over and awkwardly used my bound hands to free the key, grateful to see that it unlocked my handcuffs. I could feel the eyes—and guns—of every soldier standing on top of the wall trained on me as I stood up, tucking the cuffs and key into the side pocket of the backpack and slinging it over my shoulder. I didn't give them the satisfaction of looking back as I walked away, putting Austin behind me.

It had been a while since I'd been outside of a Safe Zone, but the streets outside of Austin looked exactly the same as the last time I'd seen them. Every building had been disused for three decades, causing them to crumble and fall. The faded shells of cars, stripped of useful parts, scattered the area. The pavement was cracked and broken, the sides littered with carcasses of both humans and mutants that had been pushed out of the way to let trucks pass. Grass and weeds sprouted between each crack, and in some places, it was difficult to see that this had once been a flourishing highway.

I'd seen pictures of what this road had looked like before the Virus hit. It had been bright and vibrant, full of people and cars and life.

Now it was a wasteland.

My throat constricted as a lone growl echoed. It was coming from a nearby building, so I set off in the opposite direction. The moment I was out of sight of the Safe Zone, I dropped to one knee and ripped open the backpack.

To my immense relief, I saw Slater had pulled through on this, at least. Alongside the key to my handcuffs and the rope, the backpack contained two pistols and some ammo, a long hunting knife, a spare change of clothes, a flashlight, matches, and as many packs of food as it could hold. The supplies wouldn't last me very long, but it was enough to get me through a day or two, enough to let me find my own supplies as I began to forge a life for myself out here.

My eyes caught on something at the very bottom of the backpack. I pulled out a piece of paper folded in half.

I balled up the note and threw it aside, wincing at what the movement did to my arm.

Silently cursing Martin and the nurse, I took a moment to inspect where the syringe had damaged my right arm. It would heal in no time, but for the moment the pain was annoying. I could feel something hard beneath my skin, like a small pellet, which was enough to make my stomach churn.

I'd worn a tracker before, a bracelet around my wrist so Slater knew where I was. Having one implanted beneath my skin was something else entirely. There was nothing stopping me from gouging it out with a knife, but that would only make my injury worse, and the tracker itself wasn't hurting anything.

My attention strayed back to the backpack. I strapped the two pistols and the knife around my waist. It had been so long since I felt a weapon in my hands that I took a moment to look over them, relishing in their familiar weight. They were all simple weapons, nothing too special, the government seal stamped on each, but they were more than enough.

The growls of the mutant grew closer. I slung the pack back over my shoulder and pressed on, my eyes scanning the buildings around me for a place to stay. It was just after ten o'clock in the morning, so I had plenty of daylight left, but the clouds gathering overhead promised rain. The last thing I wanted to do was spend my first day in exile stranded in a thunderstorm. I didn't plan on staying around Austin for very long. I knew from my time as a soldier that patrols went out all the time. If a patrol came within three hundred yards of me while I was unaware, they could use it as an excuse to shoot me. I didn't want to be anywhere near a Safe Zone so I could minimize that risk as much as possible.

Before long, I heard a shuffling of feet somewhere behind me. The mutant must be tracking my scent. I turned around, drawing one pistol as the monster limped into view.

Thirty years ago, when the Virus hit, nobody knew what the illness was or where it came from—aside from a few ill rumors that the government created it. I didn't think there had been any progress in the years since. No one had ever discovered a cure. All we knew is that the victims fell ill with flu-like symptoms, and then their skin and hair turned slimy, their bodies became distorted and ugly, and they developed a taste for human blood. Not many people had actually fallen sick with the original Virus; it was the few victims, twisted into monsters, who bit others and infected them as well. It was the widespread panic that caused neighbors to turn on each other, that caused the military to sweep in and try to clean things up by killing everyone in sight. The chaos killed more than the actual sickness did.

But now the mutants were everywhere. They were very strong, and some could be quick. The one that approached me now had a leg in shreds, causing its slow gait, but it was still deadly. My lip curled as I looked at it. It was almost as tall as me—which was saying something, given that I towered over everyone—with rotting gray skin and teeth that gleamed like shards of obsidian. Its greasy black hair hung in its eyes, which were glassy and bloodshot. The remnants of clothes hung in dirty strands around its body.

The mutant snarled at me, spit flying from its mouth as it lumbered over. I put the pistol back and drew my knife instead. Guns were loud and attracted more of the monsters. I had a limited supply of bullets as well, which meant I needed to use the knife as much as possible. I adjusted my grip on the blade as the mutant lunged. I stepped out of the way, and the mutant's momentum carried it forward. It lurched into the ground with a shriek. I plunged the knife into its back and dragged it down its spine. It writhed in pain as blood ran down its sides, forming a pool of crimson on the pavement below.

I yanked my knife out of the body and the mutant collapsed, letting out one last rattling breath before going still. Panting slightly, I wiped my knife on its leg and sheathed it. I heard more monsters growling in the distance, so I turned on my heel and headed in the opposite direction.

F O U R

Two months later…

Blood sprayed as I drug my knife through the mutant's throat. It gurgled as it fell onto its three dead companions, all of them leaking blood onto the grass. I paused, chest heaving. That made 403 kills. I noted the number in my mind as I wiped sweat off my brow.

Today marked two months since my twenty-first birthday—and two months of exile. I'd kept up a daily routine of hunting supplies, killing every mutant that crossed my path and mentally marking their deaths before moving on. The only other people I saw were a rogue band of roamers and a sole government patrol, both of which I steered clear of. I didn't need or want anybody. They would only slow me down.

My eyes scanned the area for any more mutants, but the field remained clear. I was still in Texas somewhere—at least I thought so after finding a car yesterday with a Texas license plate. I wasn't headed anywhere in particular, just wherever my travels took me. The backpack given to me upon exile was gone in favor of a bigger pack that held more supplies. I still had the same knife and one pistol. The other was broken. I'd replaced it with a rifle I had found in an old police station.

Sighing, I wiped blood from my face, sighing again as I realized it coated my arms and chest. I picked up my pack and stepped over the pile of corpses, retracing my steps to the small creek I crossed over just a few minutes before. The water was cool against my skin as I scrubbed the blood off my arms. I couldn't do much about the stains on my shirt, so I left it as it was.

The day was hot and sticky, causing sweat to drip down my spine as I started walking again, adjusting the straps of my pack on my shoulders. I had found out the hard way that the ransacked remains of cities and towns held too many mutants for me to handle on my own. In the cities, the mutants could pop out from behind a corner and swarm you, leaving you trapped between fallen buildings or ten-car pile ups that had been left to rust for thirty years. Out in the country, the mutants were harder to come by and usually traveled alone. There were also more places to run if an attack came. My goal was to kill as many of the monsters as possible, yes, but survival was higher on my list of priorities.

During my first few days of exile, I decided to make a mission of taking out the mutants. Back in Austin, killing the monsters had been considered a public service. I highly doubted anyone out here would care about my kill count, but it gave me something to work for. Something to keep me busy when nothing else sufficed.

I waded through the knee-high weeds in the field, grateful to make it to the other end without running into snakes or more mutants, both of which I detested with a fury. After clearing the line of trees on the other side, I was surprised to see I was closer to civilization than I thought. A rugged line of buildings cut across the horizon. A small town, it seemed. I checked the ammo in my guns and set off.

It took me a while to reach the town, fighting through thick undergrowth and crossing another creek that had a corpse lying face down in it. The town itself was miniscule, just a jumbled collection of stores and houses without a single living person in sight. I spotted a trio of mutants ambling down the main street. They heard my footsteps and their heads snapped towards me in unison, their greasy black hair swaying.

I had my pistol out in a flash. Three gunshots cracked through the air, silencing the nearby songbirds, and the mutants hit the crumbled pavement with a spray of blood. I holstered the gun and counted the deaths: 406.

The rest of the streets seemed quiet, free of the monsters that haunted the land. There were some signs of recent life, like warnings painted onto doors to warn of mutants trapped inside and a clean bicycle in the middle of the street, its owner long gone. I decided I didn't want to know what happened as I stepped over the bike.

I quickly discovered there weren't many things of use left in the town. Someone had already cleaned out both the grocery store and gas station. I broke into three different houses and found them in the same state. In the fourth I found three cans of soup and a half-used pack of matches.

It was getting late, so that's where I set up camp. I kindled a fire in the dust-covered mantel and spread out the sleeping bag I kept in my pack. I dug out a spoon and a can opener and got to work on a meal, heating the cans over the fire before eating them. Hunger gnawed at the insides of my stomach. It had been a while since I'd eaten a full meal, so I allowed myself two cans of soup and packed away the third.

The sun was still faintly visible over the horizon, but I was tired from a day of walking and decided to call it a night. I laid down on top of the sleeping bag. The makeshift bed wasn't even long enough to hold my tall frame, most of my legs resting on the dusty wooden floor rather than on the bag. I was more than used to it by now. The cot in my cell back in Austin hadn't been quite long enough, either.

My eyes were just closing when a scream pierced the air.

I was upright in an instant, a gun in one hand and a knife in the other. It was a female scream—a woman, probably, because it hadn't been high-pitched enough to belong to a young girl. She screamed again, and this time, I recognized the harsh snarls of mutants.

It would be so, so easy to just lie back down and ignore the screams. But I couldn't.

So I slung my rifle across my back and ran out the door, my long strides easily carrying me to the source of the ruckus.

The first thing I saw was the crowd of mutants gathered a few houses down. There were a lot of them, two dozen at least, snarling and spitting. The girl had fallen silent, and I couldn't see her. The mutants were all standing, which I took as a good sign—if they were tearing into her, they'd be on their knees with the girl pinned to the ground.

"Hey!" I shouted.

The mutants snapped their heads towards me, teeth gleaming. I gripped my blade harder as the ones closest to me lurched forward. I put them down with ease, but there was plenty more to take their places.

I grunted as I swung my knife, gutting another monster. But there were too many coming too fast. The girl—wherever she was—let out another scream. And I realized she had done it on purpose as the mutants stopped, confused by the sound coming from behind them, distracting them long enough for me to get the killing blows in.

Shouldering my way through the mutants, I finally glimpsed the girl. She had somehow scrambled to the top of one house, perched on the roof where it jutted over the porch, but the flood of mutants weighed down the rotten wood, the entire structure trembling in warning. The girl herself wore a pair of denim shorts and a tank top, her bright blue eyes wild with panic as she met my gaze. But what drew my attention was her hair.

Her waist-long hair was dyed a deep blue to match her eyes.

No wonder she had captured the attention of every mutant in Texas. That hair was bright enough to be seen a mile away—especially noticeable against the bleak remains of the town and the dull evening sky.

She yelped as the mutants pushed against the posts holding up the roof, causing it to sway. Sighing, I drew my pistol and fired at the monsters. The girl shouted, beating on the roof to distract them from me. The pistol ran out of ammo and I switched to my rifle. The mutants went down in a blaze of bullets, rivers of blood flowing through the overgrown driveway.

Silence fell. The girl let out a shaky breath, brushing her blue hair out of her eyes as she peered down at me. She didn't say a word, opting instead to gape at me from above.

I reloaded my gun, doing a silent count of the downed mutants. "Get down," I said. "That thing is about to collapse."

She didn't need to be told twice. I watched her shimmy down a drainpipe to the ground, scooping up a fallen backpack. She walked over to me, wincing as she stepped over the corpses.

Then she looked up and paused, letting out a low whistle. "Lord a'mercy. How's the weather up there?"

Her line of sight barely reached my chest. I towered over her, enough that she had to tilt her head back to look me in the eye. Her sapphire eyes surveyed me critically as she fingered the necklace around her neck, a simple silver pendant in the shape of half a broken heart.

"I know I've always been on the short side," she said, those piercing blue eyes sweeping over me, "but this is extreme. How tall are you? Seven foot?"

My eyes narrowed as she rambled on. "My name's Laiken, by the way. Laiken Lewis. Former resident of the Houston Safe Zone, exiled by choice because people didn't like me and I didn't particularly care for them, either." She winked. "But we won't have a problem with that, will we, Tall and Handsome?"

"You're welcome," I said stiffly, turning away.

"For what?"

"For saving you." I kicked a corpse, sending a mutant's head flying. "Now I'll be leaving."

Laiken whistled again. "Tall, handsome, *and* brooding. I see you're the full package."

My fingers twitched with the urge to pull out my pistol. Slater warned me against interacting with others outside the Safe Zones. Exiles were out there for a reason, all of them deemed criminals in some form or fashion. Roamers like Laiken left of their own accord and were considered crazy. And judging by the way Laiken was looking at me, I thought she might fit right into that stereotype.

I stalked away, hissing under my breath as Laiken followed.

"Thanks for saving me," she said brightly. I didn't turn and give her attention, and yet she kept talking. "This town is pretty quiet. I haven't seen a mutant in a while, but this was a pretty big herd, wasn't it? I don't know what I would have done if that roof collapsed on me. I usually stay holed up in the church down the street"—she jerked a thumb behind her, to where I had seen a small church sitting at a top of a hill on my way into town—"and it's well stocked because whoever lived there before was a doomsday prepper, if you know what I mean. That guy gathered *everything*. I only came out to get some fresh air and have a little adventure, but *boom*, I got cornered by more mutants than I've seen in the last month alone. Who would've thought?"

I dragged a hand through my hair. "Listen, Laiken, you are very welcome. I saved you, and now you are going to go back to your church, and I'll stay here, and we never have to see each other again."

She blinked. "But where's the fun in that? I'm lonely, you seem lonely, and since the universe has caused our paths to align—"

I leaned in close.

"What I mean to say," I snarled, "was *go to hell*."

Shock flared across her face, but I didn't wait around long enough to hear her reply. I stalked back down the street, leaving Laiken to stare after me.

And this time, she didn't follow.

FIVE

I awoke at the crack of dawn. It took only a few minutes to load up my supplies and prepare to leave. The last can of soup was saved for tonight, a meal to reward myself after a day's worth of hiking. If I got lucky, I would find something else to eat to hold me over before then.

I threw my pack over my shoulder and opened the door, only to stop short.

Laiken sat cross-legged on the porch, a notebook with a purple cover resting in her lap. A plastic case full of pencils and markers was next to her. She smiled at me as I froze in the doorway, my hand flying to the butt of my pistol.

"I realized," Laiken said, twirling a marker through her fingers, "that I never caught your name yesterday."

My lip curled. "If I answer, will you leave me alone?"

She shrugged. "Only one way to find out."

I wanted her gone. Immediately. Laiken was a walking target—and not to mention how much supplies, time, and effort it wasted for her to dye her hair blue. That hair was a bright blue warning sign.

"My name is Ethan," I said. "Now go away."

"Ethan, huh?" She shook her head. "I don't like that. I'm going to have to come up with a nickname for you."

"I don't want a nickname."

Laiken watched as I crossed the porch in a single stride.

"I noticed your shirt has the government seal on the back," she called after me. "Is that intentional?"

All of the clothes given to me when I was exiled had the government seal stitched on them somewhere, an eagle in flight superimposed over a black circle, the letters SZOA—standing for Safe Zones of America—written overhead. The pistol and the hunting knife had it, too. I adjusted my pack so it covered the seal on my t-shirt. "It's intentional."

"You work for the government?"

"Used to."

"What does that mean?"

I glanced back to see Laiken hovering behind me, the notebook tucked under one arm. The blue backpack from yesterday hung off of one shoulder. Her head was cocked to the side, her bright hair spilling over her shoulders.

"I was exiled," I said, the words sharp and loud.

"Why?"

I leveled my coldest stare on her. "Because I was an assassin who was betrayed, and now I'm a convicted serial killer."

I expected Laiken to back off after that, but she just rolled her eyes. "Oh, that's cool."

"I'm serious."

"Of course you are."

My fingers curled around the strap of my pack. "Why are you here? What could you possibly want from me?"

Laiken toyed with her necklace as she sauntered up to me. "I wanted to know your name, but now that I'm here, I might as well keep you company. You look lonely."

"I'm not lonely," I said, "I just want to be alone. There's a difference."

She planted her hands on her hips. "Fine then. That was

my nice way of saying that you look horrible. I was *going* to invite you back to my church for some breakfast, but if you are so hellbent on being rude, then go right ahead and leave."

I blinked at her. *Breakfast* was now a foreign concept to me. I'd gotten two meals a day in my prison cell, and because the lights never shut off and there was no clock to judge the time by, my tense of morning and night had been severely warped. Since I'd gotten out, I'd been lucky to get one meal a day in these forsaken wastelands, much less first thing in the morning. My face was now gaunt, my body lighter than I ever remembered it being.

I did not care to be around Laiken for any longer than I had to, but if what she said was true and she really was well-stocked… Well, it would be stupid of me to turn away that much supplies simply because I didn't want to interact with anyone. And since Laiken was so small and bubbly, I doubted she would—or could—try to harm me.

I angled my head. "Why are you offering?"

She lifted a shoulder in a shrug, her backpack swinging with the movement. "Like I said, you look lonely." She smiled as she brushed past me. "Now, are you coming or not?"

My mind flashed to the can of soup I was saving for supper tonight.

"I'll come," I muttered.

Laiken flashed me a sunny smile and bounded down the road. Despite it being only a few minutes past dawn, the air was already warm with the promise of a hot, humid day. Texas in the summer wasn't pleasant; soon, I'd have to start sleeping through the warm part of the day and doing my walking through the cooler nights. That's the trick people in Austin used when they had to work outside; the use of air conditioning was kept to a minimum to ration the power reserves as much as possible. There were hefty fines for those who overused their monthly power ration.

The church came into view, a plain building with a bell tower on top. It was made of bricks, which explained why it had lasted so long. It was only by the faint remains of paint clinging to the sides that I realized it had once been painted white. A crowbar was fitted through the handles of the wide double-doors, both of which were missing their latching mechanisms. The bar was there to keep mutants from entering while Laiken was away, though it would fail miserably at keeping human looters out. Laiken pulled the crowbar away with a flourish, stood aside while I entered, then closed the door and reentered the bar on the other side of the doors to lock them once again.

"Welcome to my humble abode," she announced.

The main room of the church was a treasure trove. Most of the pews were missing, the three remaining ones lined up against one wall. The rest of the room was filled with shelves teeming with trinkets of every size and shape. On the far side of the room sat a pulpit in surprisingly good condition. Behind it was the baptistry, a mural depicting mountains and pine trees overlooking a clear blue lake.

"I think the church gets its water from a well," Laiken said. "Most of the houses around here do, which means we have running water. I use the baptistry as a bath. The back rooms hold all the food and supplies." She gestured to her trinkets. "I've read the Bible a lot of times while I've been here, and I know it says to not hoard up treasures on earth, but this isn't a *hoard*, per se. I call it my museum, a monument to the beauty civilization used to have."

I looked around. None of the trinkets were very expensive; I saw several vases of fresh flowers, snow globes, pictures of random people, some cheap jewelry and dishes and paintings. It was all very *bright*, very Laiken. And she was right; I could see the theme in the items she put in here, the simple beauty in the objects she picked.

"I don't think God would mind too much," I said finally.

Laiken smiled again and said, "I'll get the food," before vanishing through a door in the back.

I walked through the church, letting my gaze roam around. My eyes fell on the stained glass windows as the sunlight peeked through them. By the time Laiken returned, I was frowning.

"Did you do this?" I asked, gesturing to the windows. They were made of normal glass, but someone had taken shards of colored glass and glued them on top, creating a fractured rainbow of colors that glittered in the early morning sun.

Laiken smiled as she nodded. "Every other church I've ever been in had stained glass windows, and it rubbed me the wrong way when this one didn't. So I took glass from old bottles and such and glued them on." She grinned. "Do you like it?"

I stepped back from the window. "You certainly put some effort into it." Effort that would have been more useful if put elsewhere.

"Sure did," she agreed. "It took—*Watch out!*"

I cursed as I accidentally backed into a shelf, knocking a vase full of flowers off. It hit the ground and shattered. I overcorrected my mishap and ended up hitting *another* shelf. This time, a snowglobe smashed into a thousand pieces as it made contact with the floor, the water inside forming a puddle at my feet.

"I'm sorry," I muttered.

Laiken gingerly guided me away from the shelves of

trinkets. "It's okay. I always expected *I'd* be the one to do that, though. I'm glad you saved me the trouble."

I watched as she knelt down, sweeping the glass into her palm with practiced carefulness. "You should have made the space between the shelves wider," I said flatly.

"I wasn't expecting a giant to come in here and wreck things," she said, giving me a dirty look. "You're like a bull in a china shop." Her face brightened, and she snapped her fingers. "That's it!"

"What?"

"Bull in a china shop," she sang. "*Bull* is a perfect nickname for you."

"*Bull?*" I asked, my brows rising.

Laiken rolled her eyes. "Let me guess, you don't like it."

"Was I supposed to?"

Mischief glinted in her sapphire eyes. "I can certainly think of some worse nicknames if you want me to."

"I'll pass."

Laiken cleaned up the mess then divided out the food. It was oatmeal. She kindled a fire in a small pit outside to heat some water, then dumped the packages of oats into the pot. The package claimed it was apple-cinnamon flavored, and while it tasted better than the cans of soup from last night, it certainly didn't taste great. Laiken, to no one's surprise, ate heartily with a smile on her face. I noticed she had strapped a pistol to her hip. It hadn't been there yesterday; either it had been in her backpack the entire time and she'd just now bothered to put it on, or she'd left it at the church during her excursion. I prayed it was the former, because I didn't want to ally myself with somebody who didn't even carry a weapon with them when they went exploring.

"So," Laiken began, scraping the last of her oatmeal from

the bottom of her bowl, "what's the plan? Where are we headed?"

"I don't know."

"Does that mean we're going to stay here while we figure it out, or does it mean we're going to wander aimlessly?"

"Take a pick," I snapped.

Laiken rolled her eyes. "Feisty, aren't we? Well, if I get to pick, I say we stay here."

"*We?* I never remember agreeing to go anywhere with you."

She raised a coy eyebrow. "You came here."

Check and mate. I suppressed a groan and ate the last few bites of oatmeal in lieu of answering.

Laiken shoved her bowl aside. "Listen, I've been out here for a while and have made sure to steer clear of any groups I saw. You are the first guy I've seen traveling alone. And since you gave me a hand with the mutants last night, that lets me know you're a good person. I don't believe that serial-killer bit for one second. If you are so determined to split ways then I'm not going to stop you. I just want you to know that I don't have any ill intentions." She bit her lip, demure for the first time. "We all need a friend."

That was a statement I didn't particularly resonate with, but I found myself holding my tongue rather than shooting it down. Laiken stared at me, her blue eyes wide and innocent. She looked incredibly well-fed for someone who claimed to have been out here for a long time.

Luke told me before I left to see about allying myself with a group. I didn't trust the people out here enough to stand being around a group of them, but Laiken was alone. Alone and loaded with supplies. *If* I were going to take on a partner, she was it.

I fiddled with my spoon. "I don't care where we go," I said finally. "I was just walking wherever the road took me and killing as many mutants as I could along the way."

"That's poetic," she teased.

"It's the truth."

She played with the hem of her shirt. "So does this mean you're going to hang around for a little while?"

"As long as you don't annoy me too much."

Laiken grinned. "No promises, Bull."

SIX

I explored the entire church, mostly to get away from Laiken, but also because I hated staying in a place I didn't know the full layout of. Besides the front doors, there were two back entrances, one of which was boarded up. The other boasted a working lock, though the door squealed like a pig when opened. It needed to be greased if I wanted to use it for a quiet getaway. None of the windows opened, and the ones in the back rooms were boarded up alongside the door.

Laiken had a scary amount of weapons, food, and supplies available, stacked in what had once been a Sunday school room. What she told me about the guy before her hoarding all the supplies was confirmed when I found a large stash of men's clothing—way too big to fit Laiken—in one room. I found the shirts fit me and quickly switched out my current bloodstained one for a fresh white t-shirt that I cut the sleeves out of, though the pants were all much too short for me to wear. I blatantly raided the rest of Laiken's stash, replacing my worn gear for new items that were just sitting unused. I didn't think she would mind too much.

I even found a map under a box full of blue hair dye and was delighted to see the approximate location of the church marked on it. We were close to the Louisiana state line in some unnamed town. The ocean wasn't far. I wasn't headed there specifically, but I'd been slowly migrating there over the last two months, and lately I'd become fond of the idea of seeing the ocean in person for the first time. I'd seen pictures, of course—Slater had an impressive collection of pictures from the pre-Virus world, the "old age," as he called it. Most showed him as a small boy, playing on a playground or swimming in the ocean or doing all the things considered normal in the old age but were nonexistent in my life. My parents told me a lot about the old age, too. I'd listened, fascinated, to every story as a kid. The only time I liked being around my parents was when they were telling me stories of old. It was the only time they really paid attention to me.

Laiken seemed like the type of person who would enjoy seeing the ocean, and I thought it would be in my best interest to go somewhere she would like, if only to get her off my back on the journey there. As long as there were mutants to kill, I didn't really care where I went or who I did it with.

I presented the map to Laiken that evening after avoiding her for most of the day. She'd spent her time working on one of her handcrafted stained glass windows, gluing shards of glass to the sole window in the church that wasn't already covered in colors.

"I thought we could go to the ocean," I said.

She studied the map. "Ooh, that would be fun, Bull. It's about a three-day walk from here."

I blinked, trying not to scowl at the use of the nickname. "You've been before?"

"From here? Yeah, a couple times." She held a piece of emerald-green glass up to the light, studying it with a critical eye. "I love swimming."

That didn't surprise me. "I'm leaving in the morning."

Laiken nodded. "Sounds like a plan."

By dawn the next morning, Laiken and I were slipping through the back door of the church. She had a better method for securing the church when she planned to be away for longer periods of time—leaving the crowbar on the inside of the main doors, slipping out the back, and locking *that* door with a chain and lock, the key to which she hid under a rock nearby. Satisfied with her work, she fanned out the map and took off, leaving me to follow silently.

Laiken marched on, her blue ponytail swinging behind her. The sun beat down with unrelenting force, and it wasn't long before my shirt was soaked through with sweat.

We stuck to the countryside. There were enough mutants who stumbled across our path that I didn't feel the need to go to a city to hunt more, and since I was freshly stocked thanks to Laiken's stash, the need for a supply run wasn't present. I would have pressed on all day if it weren't for the oppressive heat forcing us to either rest or risk heatstroke.

"So," Laiken said during one such rest, "you claim to be a killer."

"Yes." I didn't bother elaborating further.

She propped her chin up using her fist, sapphire eyes sparkling. "I would assume that you aren't talking because it's some super-secret government thing—"

"It is."

"*But,*" she continued, heedless of my interjection, "since you say you're also a *convicted serial killer*"—she raised her fingers to form air quotes—"I take that to mean that you were caught and thus your secret has been spilled."

I leveled a flat stare at her. "I don't want to talk about it."

"Right, because that would mean giving me details you don't have."

"You don't believe me?"

"Not in the slightest," she trilled. "But it makes for an interesting story, doesn't it?"

I sighed.

We went on for two days, getting up early and walking until midday, when the sun was at its peak and the day was at its hottest. We'd rest before continuing on, the shadows growing longer with every step. At night we found what shelter we could—abandoned houses and structures that looked like they could collapse at any second. Laiken would stay up for hours, the purple notebook in her lap and a marker in her hand. After a while I deduced she was drawing in it, but she never let me see her sketchbook, and I certainly didn't ask.

Everything was going well until we passed through a small group of buildings that might have qualified as a town had it not been smaller than the one I found Laiken in. I tracked down a group of mutants and killed them, bringing my total nearly to five hundred. It was on our way out of town that we passed the school—and the clearing behind it.

Laiken grinned. "It's a playground."

Stepping over the remains of a chain-link fence, I watched her run towards the rusted remnants of a swing set. Based on images I'd seen from the pre-Virus world, a playground like this would have had bright plastic slides, a set of swings, and a thick layer of mulch covering the ground. Now it was nothing more than a sad representation. The slide was gone, leaving only the stands it had rested on. The ground was a tangle of knee-high weeds. A fresh mutant corpse—complete with a horde of flies—laid in the corner of the clearing. There was only one swing still intact. It squealed pitifully as Laiken sat on it and kicked off the ground, wincing as the noise of the rusted swing shattered the silence.

"You'll attract mutants," I said.

Laiken only kicked the swing higher. The noise grew louder. "It's fun! Do you realize how long it's been since I've been on one of these?"

The land inside Safe Zone walls was too valuable to be wasted on something as useless as a playground. Austin hadn't seen a swing set in decades, though there was a set of monkey bars in the military training facility. I doubted any other city had wasted valuable property on a playground. The fact that Laiken had been on a swing before at all was shocking in itself; she must have found one somewhere outside the walls as a child.

Laiken let her feet drag on the ground, bringing herself to a stop. "You should try it, Bull," she called. Her blue eyes glowed. "It might cheer you up a little."

I stared at the narrow seat and rusted chains. It held Laiken's slender form just fine, but I would be too big. "I'd break it."

"So what? Are you going to get in trouble for it or something?"

I crossed my arms. "I don't want to break it."

A cheeky smile played across her lips. "Afraid to have a repeat of what happened at the church?"

I didn't reply.

Laiken jumped up and swaggered to my side, her eyes gleaming.

"Is the big bad bull scared of breaking a little swing?" she crooned, poking my arm.

A muscle in my jaw twitched. "I have a mission, and it does

not include playing around on a child's swing set."

"Oh, someone's grumpy."

"I feel the need to remind you that I am a *convicted serial killer.*"

She just rolled her eyes. "We should rest for a little while. I'm hot."

She waltzed back over to the swing, gracefully taking a seat and kicking it high into the air. Muttering to myself, I crossed to the little clubhouse at the center of the playset. The slide was long gone, but the stairs were mostly intact, resting in the shade cast by the clubhouse roof. It felt good to sit down. Laiken continued swinging, her bright hair flowing behind her.

I pulled water from my pack and gulped down half of it. Laiken said earlier she thought we would reach the ocean tomorrow—and she'd made sure to inform me of how excited she was to swim. I'd never swam before, but the idea of it seemed nice.

I leaned against the rails sectioning off the stairs. They were made of metal, their warmth seeping through my thin, sweat-slicked shirt, but I didn't care as I let my eyes close.

Then the snap of a twig had me bolting upright.

"Hello there, sweetheart," a man said, stepping out of the line of trees onto the playground. He didn't see me where I crouched on the stairs, observing him through the slits in the rails. He had eyes only for Laiken. She drug her feet on the ground, bringing the swing to a stop as she reached for her gun.

And for once, she wasn't smiling.

SEVEN

"Hello," Laiken said, standing up. The swing creaked behind her, swaying on a phantom breeze. "What do you want?"

The man smiled politely. "Oh, we were just passing through."

We. I gripped my pistol as two others emerged from the woods, flanking the first. "We were on a supply run," he explained, patting the bag slung over his shoulder. His smile turned vicious as he dared a step closer to Laiken. "You wouldn't have anything of use to give us, would you?"

Laiken tensed. "I'm not giving you my stuff, if that's what you're asking."

The men didn't stop walking until they stood only a foot away from her. They formed a rough semi-circle around her, intimidation at its finest. Laiken, to her credit, didn't back down an inch as she met the first man's dark gaze. His black hair gleamed in the sunlight as he angled his head at her.

"You'll want to hand over that bag, sweetheart," he purred. "We're the Vipers. We only play nice if you do."

"The Vipers, huh?" Laiken sucked on a tooth, her bravado returning. "Well, Mr. Viper, I would like for you to meet my friend. Say hi, Bull."

She gave a pointed look behind them, to where I had circled around with an assassin's grace. The Vipers turned. Their eyes widened as they tilted their heads back to look at my face, at the gun I now aimed at them.

The one with the dark hair cursed.

"Leave," I snarled, "and be thankful I don't ask for *your* bags."

The leader blinked, and the other two had the good sense to back up a step. They didn't have to know a damn thing about me, didn't have to know that I was a trained killer to realize I could wipe the floor with them in a fight. I towered over them, and with the sleeves ripped off my shirt, my muscled arms were on full display.

"I will suggest that you do what he says," Laiken said brightly. "He's very mean when he wants to be."

I bared my teeth to prove her point.

The ringleader raised his hands in surrender. "We don't want any trouble. We just saw someone who looked well off, and we wanted their stuff. It's that kind of world out here. But I see that we are outmatched, so we'll go our way, and you can go yours, and nobody has to bleed over it." He raised his hands a little further in the air. "Alright?"

I didn't believe for one second that he didn't want any trouble, but the panicked look in his eyes implied that he knew his limits in a fight. So I stepped aside, my gun still pointed in their general direction as I glowered down at them.

The trio quickly shuffled past, shooting wide-eyed looks at me over their shoulders before disappearing around the corner of the school. I stared after them for a few moments, making sure they didn't come back.

Laiken let out a low whistle. "Lord a'mercy. They're a friendly bunch, aren't they?"

It was a known fact that many of the exiles and roamers formed groups to help each other survive. There was safety in numbers, after all, especially in big cities where it was easy to get swarmed by mutants when you were alone. The man was right; it was the kind of world where the surviving groups went to war, fighting each other over supplies and food sources. Some of my work under Slater had been to break up fights between warring gangs. "We should get out of here," I said to Laiken. "If that group is big enough to have a name, then it's more than just the three of them. They're just a patrol sent out to gather supplies."

"Do you think they're the ones who did that?" she asked, jerking her chin towards the mutant corpse sprawled out by the monkey bars.

I noted the flies buzzing around it and nodded. "Probably ran across it on their way through the first time."

Which meant they knew this area well. I hefted my rifle over my shoulder and gestured to Laiken, who didn't complain as we skirted around the playground and darted into the woods.

I kept my head on a swivel long after we left the sad little town. I didn't trust the Vipers, not in the slightest. Something in the ringleader's dark gaze unnerved me. Laiken seemed to share the sentiment, because she kept glancing over her shoulder, frowning at the massive trees that surrounded us like she expected someone to pop out from behind one at any moment.

"Have you run into groups like that before?" I asked, breaking the silence that formed between us.

She lifted one shoulder in a shrug. "Sometimes. Mostly I stayed holed up in the church, watching them from the tower. Most people avoided the church at all costs—since most of you exiles are criminals, I assume they aren't very religious and thus aren't comfortable entering the house of God."

"Are you religious?"

Another shrug. "I think you're stupid not to be."

"Most people I know don't believe in God because they don't think He would punish the earth like this." I gestured around. "The Virus? The mutants? The whole apocalypse? They don't buy it."

Laiken tilted her head. "I've read the Bible a lot. God destroyed the earth with water once, and He's promised to do it again with fire. He's punished people plenty of times for not believing in Him." She shrugged for a third time. "Who's to say He hasn't found another way to punish the world for being unfaithful?"

I frowned, looking at the path ahead. "That's deep."

"Indeed." She scooped up a small leaf and twirled it between her fingers. "I think there has to be a God. The world is too intricate to not have somebody behind the scenes creating it all. There's too much hidden beauty for it all to be coincidental, for it to be a mistake. For it to all have formed out of nothing."

I thought back to Laiken's church, the vases of flowers and paintings and homemade windows of colored glass, and decided she was right.

Laiken perked up suddenly, the leaf falling from her hands to join the hundreds of leaves already scattered across the ground. "I recognize that," she said.

She pointed in front of us. I followed her finger and saw a new line of houses in the distance. Laiken was pointing towards the largest of the houses, the front of which had been covered in age-old graffiti, the multicolored paint faded with time. There were words written across the front, but time had caused the house to crumble, the windows and doors long gone, the siding peeling away, leaving only a few of the letters still intact.

Laiken skipped to the house, her blue hair bouncing with the movement.

"Does this mean we're close to the ocean?" I called after her.

"It's just a few hours away," she shouted back. I hissed as her voice echoed across the clearing, no doubt attracting every mutant nearby. "We should rest here for the night," an oblivious Laiken continued, just as loud. "We can get up in the morning and make it to the beach by midday."

In the few days I'd spent with her, I'd learned it was best to just go along with what she said. Arguing with Laiken was not a productive way to spend my time—especially since she had a way of drawing out every disagreement, twisting my words until she backed me into a corner so I was forced to agree with her. I possessed a lot of physical skills, but a silver tongue was one thing I never owned.

So I followed Laiken up the crumbling porch, scowling at the faint graffiti as she peered through the open doorway.

"There are probably mutants," I murmured.

I went to tap my gun on the doorway, a discreet way to gain the attention of the mutants in the house without attracting every one in the nearby area, but Laiken cupped her hands around her mouth and shouted, "Hey, assholes! Show yourselves!"

I suppressed a groan. A snarl sounded from deep within the house, rattling my bones. Laiken scooped up a sharp piece of lumber, the splintered remains of a porch rail, and marched into the house, following the snarl until she stumbled across a lone mutant. It was trapped underneath a fallen shelf, its blood-caked hands scrabbling on the floor, searching for purchase as its bloodshot eyes locked on Laiken.

"Aren't you sweet?" she crooned, then stabbed the rail

through its throat.

I rolled my eyes. "You can keep the next one as a pet."

She grinned. "Really? I'd prefer a dog though. Could we please—"

"No."

Laiken had the nerve to pout as she turned to view the rest of the house.

"Home sweet home," she said cheerfully.

I looked at the boarded-up windows, the tattered remains of curtains and carpet, the shattered glass, the bullet holes in the walls, the turned-over shelves and tables, the corpse sprawled on the floor with its blood forming a pool of crimson underneath it.

"Home sweet home," I deadpanned.

EIGHT

"Wake up, wake up, *wake up!*"

I cracked open my eyes to see Laiken's face not an inch from mine.

"It's time to rise and shine, Bull," she sang, pulling on my arm until I sat up. "I want to go *swimming.*"

"Get off of me," I hissed. Laiken obediently jumped to her feet and went about packing up our supplies. Sighing, I raked a hand through my dark blond hair. The last two months had allowed it to grow out, bringing it back to its normal length, the ends curling around my ears and tickling the back of my neck. While in prison, a gruff-faced guard had shaved it to my scalp every month. I finger-combed it as Laiken studied her own appearance in a cracked, dusty mirror, arranging her waist-long blue locks on either side of her face.

She *was* pretty; I had to admit. Pretty in a strange kind of way. Her piercing blue eyes had a way of looking deep into my soul, always swimming with that bright charisma she wielded as effectively as any weapon.

It was a shame I greatly disliked people like that.

Laiken barked at me to get my lazy butt up. I saw that it was nearly dawn, the sky lightening with faint traces of pink and gold and orange, so I stood up, rubbing my eyes. We ate a quick breakfast of dried food from our packs, and then we were on our way.

The day soon proved to be the hottest yet. The both of us were panting with exhaustion by the time the sun reached its peak. We entered a clearing between the trees, and I nearly sighed in relief as a breeze hit us. It was a humid breeze, but the moving air kissed my face, drying the sweat that dripped down it.

Laiken tilted her head back. "Do you smell that?" she asked excitedly.

I sniffed the air. "Salt?"

"Salt!" she agreed, bouncing on her toes. "The ocean!"

Right. We had to be nearby, then. I was prepared to take a rest, but Laiken was already running, following the breeze. I caught up to her easily, my long strides closing the distance between us right before we cleared the line of trees, revealing a glittering blue expanse before us.

The ocean. I sucked in a breath as I took it in. The vast expanse of deep blue-green water extended towards the far horizon. A long stretch of beach outlined it, the sand dissolving into boulders and rocks before disappearing into the line of trees Laiken and I now stood in.

Laiken's grin was as bright as the sun. "We're here!" she said, leaping onto a boulder. She picked her way across the rocks, stopping once to see if I followed.

And when she did, a wicked grin split her face.

"This is the first time I've been able to look you in the eye," Laiken giggled.

Indeed. With her on the rock and me on the ground, it made up for the height difference between us. I scowled. "Stop looking so happy about it."

"Fine. Since I'm your height, I might as well act like it." She folded her arms over her chest, matching my scowl with one of her own. "Is this better?"

I stalked for the beach, shooting her a glare over my shoulder.

No picture had prepared me for the utter vastness of the ocean, the endless water stretched out before me as I reached the edge of the shore. In Slater's photos, the beach was crowded with people, boats floating in the distance. Neither was present now, but I preferred it that way. It was quiet. Calm. Peaceful.

Laiken chucked her bag to the ground and kicked off her shoes. I blinked as she peeled off her shorts and tank top, revealing a polka-dotted bathing suit underneath.

I choked. "You've been wearing that this entire time?" She must have been burning up.

"I changed this morning," she explained, tying back her hair. Then, without further warning, she ran into the water, stopping only when it came up to her chest. "Come on, Bull," she called, splashing water in my direction. "It's refreshing!"

I dropped my pack next to hers. I didn't have a proper swimsuit, but I did have a pair of shorts, so I ducked behind the rocks to change. Laiken waved at me to hurry up as I stepped to the edge of the water, barefoot and bare-chested.

"Come *on*, Bull," she said again. "Don't make me call you Chicken."

The water lapped against my toes. I took a tentative step forward, wading through the water until I was waist-deep. It made me feel oddly light—something I wasn't used to. More than that, it was *cool*, just as refreshing as Laiken claimed. I scooped some in my hands and splashed my face, wincing as some got into my mouth and the taste of salt caused my lips to pucker.

Laiken dunked under the waves. Her hair swirled around her, nearly blending in. When she came back up, her dripping hair hanging in her face, she took one glance at me and frowned.

"Is something wrong?" she asked.

I shrugged. "I don't—I mean—" I coughed. "I've never gone swimming before."

"Oh?" She swam towards me. "You aren't scared, are you?"

I shrugged again, not liking the mischievous gleam in her eyes. "I'm not scared. I just—"

"Don't know how?"

"Let me guess," I gritted out. "You're going to offer to teach me?"

"It's a good thing I'm such an *amazing* teacher," Laiken trilled, splashing me. "I can't believe you don't know how. Swimming is a must-have skill for anyone who claims to be an assassin-slash-serial killer."

My eyes narrowed. "I don't need a teacher."

"Don't you?"

"No." I waded further out and ducked under the water, soaking my hair. When I emerged, Laiken was giving me a dirty look, her hands on her hips.

"I'm just trying to help you," she said stubbornly.

"Well, you aren't," I snapped, and something like hurt flashed in her eyes.

"Fine," she retorted, swimming away from me. She dove underwater again and stayed under for long enough that I became mildly worried. Then she popped back up, her hair falling out of its ponytail and sticking to her face and neck. She ignored me as she kicked out further to sea.

I watched her flip over, floating on her back. Her eyes even fluttered to a close, the picture of peace and relaxation. It set my teeth on edge. She *did* know how to swim.

I turned away before my traitorous mind could convince me to take her up on her offer.

We swam for hours. Or rather, Laiken swam while I stood awkwardly in the water, occasionally splashing myself to keep cool.

The sun inched towards the horizon, so I called it quits. We needed to find shelter before nightfall. The mutants were hard enough to fight in the day; fighting them in the dark, when their gray skin and inky hair blended into the night, was another battle altogether.

Laiken had warmed back up to me, it seemed, her usual smile suggesting all was forgotten. "I know a place," she said. The way she said this, her voice bright, had me a bit worried she was going to lead me into a trap to take out her anger, but I found myself following her into a large house about fifteen minutes away from where we swam.

It was very nice, I noted, a mansion near the beach. The brick structure had held up nicely over the years, the wide doors in surprisingly good condition. The windows were even intact, barely even warped or discolored. The yard was unkempt. Weeds and some kind of vine overtook the porch, the plants draping off the rails and posts and roof. They tickled my head as I walked past. Laiken hunted through an over-flowing flower pot to the right of the porch, eventually emerging with a rusty house key in her hand and a smile on her face.

"You've been here before," I noted as she unlocked the door.

Laiken nudged it open with her foot, tucking the key into the pocket of her denim shorts. "I said I knew a place."

She sauntered inside. I followed, ducking my head to fit through the doorway. We walked through the foyer and entered a spacious living room, sheets covering the furniture, the floor covered in a thick layer of dust.

I let out a low whistle as I kicked the door shut behind me. "I'll consult you the next time I plan a vacation."

"Oh yes," Laiken agreed, flipping her still-wet hair over her shoulder. "I know every hidden gem from here to Houston." She dropped her pack on the couch, kicking up a cloud of dust that caused her to sneeze. "It needs a little cleaning, though. You can't even tell I was here before."

"How long ago was it?"

She shrugged. "A year, maybe? I lose track of the days."

My mind flashed back to my prison cell. There had been no windows or clocks to judge the time by, only Luke coming whenever he was on shift and telling me what day it was. I had only been there for six months, but it felt like years. "It's easy to do that."

"Yeah," Laiken murmured. There was a touch of sadness in her voice, a hollow feeling that echoed in my mind. I wondered, not for the first time, what had brought Laiken out here, what had prompted her to leave the Safe Zones.

Former resident of the Houston Safe Zone, exiled by choice because people didn't like me and I didn't particularly care for them, either, is what she told me when we first met. It was the only explanation she'd given as to why she'd chosen life as a roamer. Not many wanted to brave the wastelands by choice; most of the people out here were either exiles like myself, or they had simply been surviving in the wastelands since the beginning of the Virus and they'd never bothered seeking out the Safe

Zones for help. Luke's family had been the latter—he'd come to the Zones after a herd wiped out his parents and siblings when he was young, forcing him to find help.

Laiken disappeared through a wide doorway into what looked like a dining room, a kitchen beyond it. I dropped my pack to the floor and sighed at the ceiling. Laiken was a mystery I was determined to solve, one way or another.

NINE

By the end of the night, Laiken had completed two hours' worth of housekeeping. She rearranged furniture, hung sheets over the windows as makeshift curtains, cleared debris, and even went as far to give the living room floor a rudimentary mopping. I watched her from where I sat in the corner, organizing my bag and taking stock of what I had. She just hummed to herself as she worked, never quite meeting my gaze, though I felt her eyes on me every time my head was turned away.

The idea of leaving and heading back to Laiken's church to take the remainder of her supplies came to my mind at some point in the night. It wouldn't be difficult; I could slip out while she was asleep and make the trek back. My stamina and speed would easily outmatch hers. I could have the church raided and be long gone a full day before she came back. It was a devilish thought, the kind that made me squirm to think about—which surprised me because I was an *assassin*. I'd slit throats without batting an eye. Why was the idea of screwing Laiken over bothering me so much?

I didn't sleep very well that night.

Laiken was once again awake before me, which irritated me. I didn't trust her. She was too happy, too bright, too…*fun*.

It was unsettling.

I watched her now as she skipped throughout the house,

humming to herself as she picked up last night's cleaning spree. The church had been spotless before we left, and I suspected Laiken made a hobby out of keeping things clean. The wastelands were covered in filth; Laiken seemed like the type of girl to want to clear that filth away.

She continued humming a little tune as she all but danced through the living room. She caught my stare and grinned. "I see you're awake, sleepyhead."

I clenched my jaw as I stood up. "Yeah."

"I like it here," she said, gesturing around her. "I think we could stay here for a while, if it's alright with you."

"Really?"

She bobbed her head in confirmation. "It needs a little work, but I like a good project. I'm sure there'll be plenty of mutants for you to kill around here." She shrugged. "Though I don't really see the point in it. Seems like a waste of time killing mutants when there's only going to be more of them."

"The government considers it to be a public service."

Laiken waved a hand. "Government, shovernment. They don't know what the heck they're doing."

"What makes you say that?"

"It's been thirty years since the Virus struck, and all they've managed to do is build a bunch of fancy walls and figure out a way to communicate between them. They've made no progress in rebuilding America or reestablishing connections with the rest of the world. We're just assuming that everyone is as bad off as we are and that they're keeping to themselves, but for all we know, some European nation is slowly overtaking our coast." She gestured wildly. "And tell me you've heard the theory about the government creating the Virus in the first place."

"I never took you for a conspiracy theorist."

"It's not a conspiracy," she said solemnly.

"You have no idea what you're talking about," I said. "I worked for the government."

"And look where it landed you," she mused. "You claim to be an exiled serial killer who spends his time killing mutants and getting annoyed by me." She winked. "Not that I'm complaining."

I gritted my teeth and said nothing more.

Laiken took my silence to mean that she won the debate and sauntered into the kitchen. "I think we should stay here," she called over her shoulder, idly flipping through her sketchbook, which had been left on the counter. "It's a nice place, and it won't take more to secure it. And if I remember right, there's a town nearby. Could be a lot of mutants there for you to deal with."

Once again, I found myself weighing the pros and cons of sneaking out and raiding Laiken's church. But she was looking at me with a hopeful gaze, that damn smile still on her face, and I realized I couldn't go through with it. As much as she annoyed me, Laiken wasn't a bad person. Hell, she was the polar opposite of a bad person. She'd handled herself for however long she'd been in the wastelands, and who was I to throw away such expertise? I doubted she would try and strangle me in my sleep. She was so small compared to me that she didn't pose much of a physical threat. And whatever had happened yesterday, when she seemed a bit angry at me, had vanished entirely.

I couldn't bring myself to leave her. So I said, "We'll check it out tomorrow."

Laiken grinned in answer.

"I'm going to fix this place right up," she said. "It'll be fun."

I had a feeling there were a lot of things Laiken considered as *fun*. "I'm not helping you decorate."

She snickered. "Oh, I wouldn't dream of it. I have a different job for you."

"Oh?"

"I need a big, strong man to help me fix the foyer," she said, steering me towards the room in question. Cracks of daylight shone through the trim beside the doors and windows. None of it looked very secure. "If a mutant comes up here, it might just smash its way inside. We don't want that to happen, do we?"

And that's how I found myself rummaging through the neighboring houses a few hours later, searching for supplies to fix the foyer.

I actually enjoyed the job more than I let Laiken know. The houses had a lot of mutants in them, trapped under fallen furniture or in cracked floorboards, all of them easy to kill. I wasn't a fix-it kind of guy, but I didn't think it would take much to reinforce the door and windows, and once I got started scrounging up boards and pieces of metal to do it with, I had to admit it felt good to do something with my hands that didn't involve bloodshed.

It was nice.

I stumbled across a kid's red wagon in the first house I checked. The metal body was rusted beyond repair, but three of the wheels were still in good enough condition for it to roll without much trouble. I chucked all the materials I found inside. Most everything was rotted or rusted, but I scrounged up the best-looking pieces. Laiken would be sorely disappointed if she was counting on me to do a bang-up job. I'd secure the door and window frames, keeping the mutants out, but it would not look pretty.

I found a toolkit in the last house. A spider had made its home inside, the hammers and screwdrivers covered in cobwebs, but I selected what I needed and chucked it into the wagon. I headed back towards the house Laiken commandeered for us. The wagon was made for a child, which meant the handle was also made for someone half my size, forcing me to stoop down to pull it behind me. I lumbered along, the wheels of the wagon squealing as it bounced and rattled along the cracked, weed-ridden pavement. A particularly nasty weed tangled into one wheel, pulling the entire operation to a halt.

Grumbling to myself, I dropped to one knee to fix the wheel. The jerk from stopping pulled one screw loose, so I fished out the screwdriver and went about fixing it.

"I'm just your average handyman now," I muttered under my breath.

The faint echo of voices had me freezing. I was on my feet in an instant, kicking the wagon into the shallow ditch on the side of the road as I darted for cover. I flung myself into the shadows cast by a porch just as the voices became louder and three figures emerged down the street.

Three figures I recognized.

The Vipers.

"I swore I heard something out this way," the one in the middle was saying. I identified him as the leader from last time, his jet-black hair gleaming in the Texas sun. He wore a t-shirt and shorts, his companions wearing similar outfits. The three of them looked as travel-worn as I had felt yesterday. I wasn't much better off today; I'd spent most of the last few hours out of the brutal sun, but the insides of the houses were hot and stuffy, the walls blocking the regular movement of air.

"I heard something," the guy on his left confirmed. He had

blond hair, lighter than my own.

The final, brown-skinned man mumbled, "I didn't hear a thing."

"Someone's here," the first announced.

"It could have just been a mutant."

"Have you *seen* a mutant, Josh?"

"Have you *seen* a *person*, Nico?" the dark-skinned one—Josh—fired back.

Nico's dark eyes narrowed on his companion. "The girl and the giant have to be around here somewhere. Find them, or I'll have your head."

TEN

I sucked in a breath as Josh and the unnamed Viper exchanged a look, then split off in different directions. Nico continued glaring down the street long after they disappeared from view.

The girl and the giant. My lip curled. He was looking for Laiken and I; how they had followed us this far, hours away from the place we first encountered them at, was beyond me. They'd tracked us somehow. I couldn't see any signs of the heavy packs they had when we first ran into them on the playground. Their base must be near that town. They dropped off their stuff, then immediately came back to hunt us—and our supplies—down.

The Vipers had come from the direction of where our hideout was, where I had been heading before I heard them coming. They hadn't found Laiken yet. The noise of the wagon was probably what caught Nico's attention.

If they tried to raise a finger against me, I would rip their heads off and feed their bodies to the mutants.

Silent as a mouse, I circled around the house, giving the Vipers a wide berth. I left the wagon full of supplies behind, overturned in the ditch. We needed more than reinforcements against the monsters.

I burst through the door of our hideout. Laiken was nowhere to be seen. I hissed her name, and she called brightly from the kitchen, "I'm in here!"

I lunged for the kitchen. Laiken was at the table, doodling in her sketchbook. She opened her mouth but I slapped my hand over it before she could get a word out. Her eyes widened in confusion, her body going tense as I dragged her into the living room.

"The Vipers from the other day are here," I hissed. "Hunting us. *Be quiet.*"

I released her. To her credit, Laiken seemed unruffled, but it did not escape my notice how she drew the pistol at her side and checked how many bullets were in it. I'd brought my knife and gun with me to search for supplies, but now I shouldered my rifle.

"What do we do?" Laiken asked, her voice barely above a whisper.

"They're trying to find us. I don't know how, but they know—or at least suspect—that we're in this area." I cocked the gun. "I intend to find them first."

Her blue eyes went wide. "So you're going to go all serial-killer on them?"

Her tone was entirely too enthusiastic. I narrowed my eyes. "Yes, Laiken. I'm going to go all serial-killer on them."

I strode for the door. Laiken bounded after me.

"You shouldn't come with me," I said over my shoulder. "I can convince them that we split up—it's safer for you that way."

"Don't care," she said. "I want to see this."

I pinched the bridge of my nose and let out a long sigh.

Laiken trailed me all the way to where I had last seen the Vipers. They were gone now. Motioning to be quiet, I led Laiken to the house I'd taken refuge behind. We crept through the overgrown backyards until we heard Nico's annoying voice again, his anger made clear even before we could make out the words.

"...got to be here somewhere," he snarled. It sounded like he was standing in front of the nearest house. I slid forward. "I tracked them here!"

"Maybe you misread it," the other Viper said. "I know the mutant prints look different, but there are other people here somewhere."

Nico snorted. "The giant has enormous feet. There's no mistaking the prints."

Laiken's lips quirked into a smile as she glanced down at my boots, as if to say that my feet were, indeed, very big. I glared at her.

Nico continued his rant. It seemed the Vipers were taking a rest, the heat of the day finally getting to them. I leaned over to Laiken and murmured, "Stay hidden. I'll take care of them."

"I want to help," she said.

"You're my backup," I reassured her, but the plan was to not need any. I leaned my rifle against the side of the house. My feet, however big they were, remained silent as I crept through the tall grass. I peered around the side of the house and found Nico and the other Vipers standing on the remains of the porch, taking advantage of the shade. Josh was sitting down, fanning himself with a folded map. I eased to my knees and army-crawled the last few feet to the front of the porch.

The Vipers didn't know what was happening until I was already on them.

I leapt up the stairs, my fist sailing right into the back of the blonde's head. He fell into the railing and did not rise. Nico's eyes widened with recognition. He let out a yell and charged. I took the brunt of his attack with my shoulder, knocking him back. He slammed into a post with a grunt. Josh finally made it to his feet. My fist cracked across the Viper's face, sending him flying. Nico lunged again, but this time, I noticed the gun in his hand.

Cursing, I threw myself to the side as a bullet flew past my ear. "Not so high and mighty now, are we?" Nico sneered. "Where's your little sweetheart? Three against one seems awfully unfair."

Josh stumbled to his feet, holding his bloody nose. The other remained unconscious. I made to draw my pistol, but Nico cut me off with a click of his tongue.

"One move," he warned, "and I'll pump you full of lead, you big oaf."

I raised my bloody fist, prepared to deliver another blow, the gun be damned, but Laiken's voice had the Vipers coming to a halt.

"I'm going to advise you to step away, *sweetheart*," she drawled, spitting that nickname right back in his face. I peered over Nico's shoulder to see her standing behind the Vipers, holding my rifle, her foot tapping impatiently as she aimed it between Nico's shoulder blades. "You'd do good just to mosey on out of here before *I* pump *you* full of lead."

Nico tried to turn. Laiken hissed in warning, and he went still as she switched off the safety.

"My friend there has a very big gun," I said, "and she's got it aimed at you. I suggest you drop that weapon before she does something nasty."

His dark eyes narrowed. I met Laiken's gaze, and she gave me a shallow nod.

"Turn around," she ordered.

Nico and Josh didn't turn all the way, but the twist of their heads was enough for me to jump at them, knocking the pistol out of Nico's hand and sending both of them crashing to the ground. I slammed my boot onto Nico's chest, drawing a sharp breath from him.

Laiken gracefully ascended the porch steps, her fingers tapping the rifle as she came to stand beside me. She flashed Nico a cheeky smile as he glowered at us. I leaned down a bit more, putting more of my considerable weight on his chest.

"Who do you think you are?" I demanded.

His eyes gleamed. "Nico De La Cruz," he spat. He somehow managed to peer down his nose at us despite being sprawled on the ground. "I am the leader of the Vipers."

"Well, not so high and mighty now, are we?" Laiken said cheerfully.

His lip curled. "And who are you?"

Laiken happily supplied her name. "Ethan Ellis," I said, waiting to see if any recognition crossed his face. I doubted the Vipers had heard about me—I suspected they had left the Safe Zones long before my name made the news—but I threw my full name out there all the same. Nico's face remained impassive. He didn't recognize me. Laiken glanced at me, but she didn't react to it, either.

Nico grunted as I pressed down harder on his chest. "This is your only warning," I said, my voice soft. "You came here to hunt us, but you were hunted down instead. We knew exactly where to find you." An exaggeration of the truth, but I was determined to put these wretched Vipers off our trail for good. Intimidation was the best way to accomplish that. "Next time, we won't play so nice. If you try to track us again, you will find yourself spiked to the ground while a horde of mutants rips you limb from limb." My boot dug in harder. "And you'll be conscious to feel every damn second of it. Do I make myself clear?"

Nico only snarled in response.

I leaned down and growled right in his face, *"Do I make*

myself clear?"

I'd seen Slater employ that tactic enough times to know that this Nico De La Cruz would cave. He finally dropped my gaze, hissing an affirmation under his breath. I stepped off of him. Nico remained down, but I didn't trust him in the slightest, so I kicked him in the face for good measure. His head jerked to the side, a bruise blooming across his jaw. *How's that for enormous feet?* I thought smugly.

Josh gaped at his two unconscious friends, then back up at me.

"Make sure he knows not to follow me again," I snarled.

He nodded emphatically. I scooped up the fallen guns, and with one last glare at the Vipers, Laiken and I made our exit. We hit the street and began walking in the opposite direction of where we were staying, waiting until we were out of sight to cut through the backyards once again and head to our hideout. It was only once we were safely behind closed doors did Laiken blow out a long breath.

"You sure do know how to threaten someone," she said.

"It's easy when you mean every word of it."

She sauntered to my side. "Is that what it looks like for you to go all serial-killer on somebody?"

I didn't answer her question, opting instead to take my rifle back and make sure the safety was on. "That's not the last we've seen of them," I said. "I think they'll go back to whatever hole they came from, but that Nico character…"

"Nico?"

"The leader. I've met people like him before. He didn't like being put down like that. The moment he wakes up, he'll start plotting his revenge. It might not be today, or even this week, but eventually he'll be back with as much manpower as he can scrounge up." My hands curled into fists. "He won't forget.

He's got a grudge now, and he'll want to make us pay."

Laiken crossed her arms. "Does that mean we should leave? Can we even get away? How did he find us to begin with?"

"He's a tracker," I said. "He can make out footprints in the dirt and shit like that. It's mostly pavement through here, so I don't think he can figure out the exact house we're at, but he was able to track us to this general area."

"Which brings us back to my question: should we leave?"

My jaw clenched as I stared out the window, as if Nico would come swaggering to us at any moment, ready to end this here and now.

"No," I said at last. "We can handle him."

A worried frown pulled at Laiken's lips, but then she shrugged it off with a light, "If you say so," then plopped down in a chair as if everything were perfectly normal.

My gaze returned to the window, and there was only one thought in my mind.

I should have killed them.

ELEVEN

I never ended up reinforcing the door and windows that day. The wagon of supplies I collected was still in the ditch, and with the Vipers still nearby, I didn't feel good about my chances of getting it back undetected—especially not when the wheels squealed loudly enough to attract the attention of anyone within a two-mile radius.

I spent the rest of the afternoon on high alert, stalking from window to window, looking for any sign of the Vipers, my hand never straying too far from the trigger of my gun. I saw no one. In the morning, Laiken and I ventured outside to do a sweep through the neighborhood.

"I'm not seeing anyone," she said.

The first house we checked was the one where we'd left Nico and his friends the day before. They were gone. The only sign they'd been there to begin with was the busted railing I'd thrown the unnamed Viper into, and some splatters of blood that probably came from the nosebleed I'd given Josh. I scanned the surrounding area, but I was not a skilled tracker like Nico was, so I wasn't able to spot any footprints or subtle signs that suggested which way they went.

"There's nobody here," I agreed at long last.

We combed every house on the street. It took us all day, but I fell asleep that night feeling much more secure after confirming that the Vipers weren't nearby. The event seemed to have subdued Laiken as well. She was much more quiet than usual, and while she flashed her usual smile every time I met her gaze, a concerned expression replaced it whenever she thought my back was turned.

"I'm going to check out the city today," I said in the morning over our meager breakfast of canned fruit. I suspected most of Laiken's supplies were taken from the Safe Zones; even non-perishable food didn't last this long when left to rot inside of abandoned houses or stores. The Safe Zones contained factories and gardens to produce food, and many fenced off nearby sections of farmland for mass production. The goods were distributed evenly among the Safe Zones. Austin didn't have much in that regard—as the post-Virus capital, it was home to the workings of the government. The only people that lived there regularly were government workers and their families and significant others. The city got its food imported from nearby Zones. Many such deliveries were the target of roamers and exiles who raided the trucks for food and supplies. Hordes of mutants also sometimes caused the trucks to crash. If left alone, someone would eventually come by and ransack the vehicle for its precious cargo. It was an elusive business, one that the previous owner of Laiken's church had taken advantage of.

"Do you want me to come with you?" Laiken asked.

I nodded my head. I'd poured over the map many times, finally pinpointing our location near a city called Freeport. My search for mutants aside, I thought it was potentially a place where the Vipers could have snuck off to in order to heal. They'd all been injured; they might have left the immediate area, but I found it hard to believe they'd gone very far. I wanted to find them, to kill them before the problem got any worse. Laiken would be another set of eyes to help look for them. That, and if Nico had somehow found our location, I didn't want to leave her alone. Slater would shake his head at me for caring so much about someone who offered me relatively little in return—my protection was benefiting Laiken more than her company was benefiting me—but since Slater hadn't held up on his promises, I found myself not caring in the slightest about what he might think.

He's the one who allowed me to be exiled. He couldn't complain about what I did now.

It didn't take long to reach Freeport, even though we took precautions by keeping as hidden as possible, sticking to the woods and backroads. Laiken paused several times to pick up shards of glass from the ground, tucking them into a jar in her backpack. I didn't ask what they were for, though I suspected it was for her stained glass windows back at the church. When we reached the city, the snarls of mutants greeted us, echoing from deeper within.

"This place gives me the chills," Laiken said, hugging herself. Her blue hair and skin-tight purple tank top were obscenely bright against the gritty remains of the city. If the Vipers were here, they would have no problem spotting us.

"Welcome to the wastelands," I deadpanned.

She rolled her eyes. "You're a real charmer, you know that?"

I snorted. "In what world am I a *charmer?*"

"Oh, it's in there somewhere." She rose up on her tiptoes to pat me on the shoulder. "It's just buried deep. You're a genuine diamond in the rough."

"Diamond in the what?"

"Rough." She cocked her head to the side. "You've never heard that before?"

"I have no idea what you're talking about," I said.

Laiken planted her hands on her hips. "*Diamond in the rough?* It's a saying? A figure of speech?" At my still-confused expression, she sighed dramatically and elaborated, "You poor, uneducated thing. It means there's something good underneath all that bad."

"You're saying I'm bad?"

"What I'm *saying*," Laiken said, "is that you appear not-so-nice on the outside, but inside you have a heart of gold." She poked my arm. "You just refuse to show it."

I stared at her. "Once again, I am a *convicted murderer.*"

"You keep saying that, and yet I have not witnessed such a thing."

And with that last jab, Laiken ambled into the city, her hands stuffed into the pockets of her shorts.

I was beginning to think God sent Laiken to me as a test of patience.

I followed Laiken down the street, twisting at every noise. Mutants—a lot of them—were nearby, but they had yet to show themselves. Laiken didn't even break stride. I frowned after her as she read the signs on every building we passed, as if she were looking for one in particular.

And apparently, that's exactly what she was doing, because eventually she stopped and declared, "This is the one."

It was a sporting goods store. I took up a position next to Laiken, my shadow swallowing hers, and asked, "Do you need anything in particular?"

For a moment, I was terrified she was going to say she needed feminine products, but Laiken just tossed her hair over her shoulder.

"It's not what *I* need," she said ominously. "It's what *you* need."

"And what is that, exactly?" I growled as she walked into

the store.

Laiken didn't answer right away. She stepped through the front door, which once had been made of glass but now was nothing more than a metal frame and some shards on the ground. Mutants growled from within. Grumbling to myself, I ducked through the door and drew my knife, bracing myself as three of the monsters appeared from the shadows.

Three slashes of my blade had them hitting the ground. 515 kills. By the time I looked up again, Laiken was already disappearing behind the rows of shelves.

"Please tell me what we're doing here," I called after her. My voice echoed. A mutant snarled from somewhere to my left, accompanied by a heavy rattling sound. It didn't come any closer, so I assumed it was trapped, at least for the time being.

I jogged after Laiken, stepping over fallen merchandise covered in a layer of dust, ducking underneath a light suspended in the air by nothing but a bundle of wires. When I finally caught up to her, I stopped short, scowling as I realized what section she sought out.

Swim gear.

"I thought this might help you," she said, her gaze innocent as she nudged a pool noodle in my direction. The store boasted a massive selection of swimwear and gear, all of it untouched despite the years. It was all nasty, covered in cobwebs and dust, the plastic packaging worn down by time. Some items were stained with something that looked suspiciously like blood.

My gaze slid to Laiken. "You can't be serious."

"I have never been more serious in my entire life," she said solemnly, though the act quickly vanished as a smile broke out over her face. "Come on, Bull! It'll be fun! I can teach you how to swim and then we can play around in the ocean all day—"

"Laiken," I snapped. She closed her mouth. "I did not come here to look at bathing suits."

"There are also floaties."

"*Laiken.*"

"Alright, alright," she muttered, holding up her hands in mock surrender. "Chill out. I was just trying to help you out. My sister taught me how to swim in a big creek outside the Safe Zone. She always said that it was a necessary skill because it might, you know, *save your life one day.*" She shrugged, feigning nonchalance. "But if you don't want to, that's fine."

I pinched the bridge of my nose. If the Vipers could see us now, I doubted they would feel near as threatened by our presence. Laiken, innocently using her foot to push a box with a unicorn floatie in it towards me while I glared down at her.

What a pair we made.

"Let's get out of here," I said.

Laiken let out a soft sigh, but she trailed after me without further protest. The mutant I heard earlier untangled itself and came lurching at us; I sliced its throat open without breaking stride.

A thick layer of clouds covered the sky, giving us a merciful reprieve from the unrelenting sun. This morning, the sky had been a light dove gray—now, as afternoon approached, it had darkened considerably, the near-black clouds seeming to press down from above. A storm was on the way. I wouldn't mind a little rain, not when the grass was starting to wither and the ground underneath it starting to crack, when the creek Laiken and I fetched water from was only a few days from drying up completely, but I prayed the storm wouldn't be too devastating. There weren't many solid houses left to hole up in if a natural disaster struck. The apocalypse hadn't stopped the tornadoes and hurricanes.

I told Laiken as much, and she said she was fairly sure our hideout had a basement.

"Fairly sure?" I echoed.

She nodded. "There was a door. With some steps that went down. But it was dark and kind of scary down there, so we're just going to assume there's a basement for a time being."

"But we don't know for sure."

"I'm ninety-nine percent sure that any stairs that go below the first floor lead to a basement."

"But we don't know if it's usable," I retorted. "Who knows if we can even get to it?"

Laiken bit her lip.

I sighed. "We need to get back before the storm hits, at least." I didn't want to be traveling with a storm brewing overhead—thunder lured mutants out of hiding, and it was hard to see them in heavy rain. I learned that lesson the hard way during my first few days of exile.

As if summoned by my thoughts, a lone mutant stumbled out into the street ahead of us.

Laiken drew a knife and angled it at the monster. "Well, let's kick some mutant butt and get out of here before the rain comes."

And that was perhaps the most sensible thing I'd ever heard her say.

TWELVE

We killed the mutant. And the one that came after it. And the next. And then the small herd that lumbered over after being attracted by the noise of their comrades dying.

We cleared the entire street by the time the first raindrop landed on my face.

I swore as I watched the droplets form small dots on the pavement. I hadn't expected the rain to come so soon.

"We need to get out of here," Laiken said, frowning as she held her arm out, feeling the rain that landed there. "It'll take us longer to get back in the rain."

We froze as a fork of lightning danced across the sky.

I saw Laiken silently mouthing *one, two, three…* all the way to ten, when a ground-shaking rumble of thunder rattled me to the core.

Laiken glanced at me and reported, "The storm is two miles away."

I started walking. "How'd you figure that out?"

"The number of seconds between the lightning and the thunder, divided by five. It's called the flash-to-bang technique." She began walking faster as a second lightning strike illuminated the sky, which was growing darker by the minute. "I might suggest we start running."

And so we did, breaking into a jog as the rain picked up. I cursed as thunder rumbled again. By the time we made it out of

Freeport, my blonde hair was plastered to my face, my clothes soaked through with water.

"Faster," Laiken panted.

She burst into a full-on sprint. I could have run faster than her, but I made myself slow down, keeping pace with her to not lose her as the rain pelted down. My range of visibility was cut short as the storm thickened.

A shape moved in front of me. I paused, brushing my wet hair out of my eyes as I squinted ahead, trying to see if it was a person or just a tree blowing in the wind.

And that's when Laiken screamed.

"Laiken!" I whipped around, but she was nowhere to be found. I turned in a full circle, trying to see her through the downpour. The world had turned into a mess of rain and wind and lightning, the trees and buildings nothing but vague gray shapes. I shouted her name again, but the wind ripped away the sound. Rain lashed at me from every side. Confused and panicked, I came to a stop, panting for breath.

The shape I saw earlier lurched for me—a mutant. I barely had time to react as it slammed into me. I shoved it off, my lip curling at the feel of its rotten skin, made slimy by the rain. I drew my knife and stabbed it in the heart, taking off running before the body hit the ground.

"*Laiken!*" I shouted again.

"*Ethan!*"

I dove for the sound. Laiken had only used my name once before, opting to call me *Bull* instead, so the fact she used my real name—alongside the sheer desperation and panic in her voice—had me hurtling towards her without a second thought.

I nearly crashed into her. She leaned against a tree, panting, the corpse of a mutant at her feet. Her knife was buried up to the hilt in its neck. Her blue hair, dripping with water droplets, hung in her face.

I grabbed her by the shoulders, shocking her. "Are you okay?" I demanded.

She was shaking. "I'm—I'm alright. It just came out of nowhere and it scared me—"

"Are you bitten?"

"No." Her voice trembled, but her eyes remained steady. "I'm okay."

Lightning flashed overhead, momentarily illuminating our surroundings—including the mutant approaching us from the side. "Shit," I spat, dragging Laiken away. Fighting the monsters in the rain was not a wise choice. We needed to get the hell out of here.

One hand on Laiken's shoulder to make sure she didn't slip away again, I picked a direction and started running. I had no clue where we were. I just ran until I saw the vague shape of a building ahead, four walls and a roof that would offer us any sort of relief from the storm.

We tumbled inside. I slammed the door shut behind us, and Laiken sank to the floor. It was not a house I recognized, but the shadows and flashes of lightning had a way of twisting the world, so I couldn't be sure. A mutant shuffled down the hallway towards us; I drew my gun and shot it, not caring about the noise, not when the thunder would most likely drown it out.

"Are you okay?" I asked Laiken again, taking a seat next to her.

A puddle had already formed underneath her. She shivered, wrapping her arms around herself as she stared out the open window, where the storm raged at full force. We were far enough down the hall to be away from the spray of rain, but the wind still reached us. I positioned myself between Laiken and the window, blocking as much of it as I could.

"I don't know," she said at last. She rubbed her arm. "I'm not hurt, it's just… It got close back there." She let out a bitter laugh. "I almost died. That mutant was coming for me and if I hadn't already had my knife in my hand—"

"You didn't die," I said softly.

Her throat bobbed. "Yeah. I guess that's what matters, isn't it?" This statement seemed to strengthen her, to bring some of the light back into her eyes. "It's what matters most," she echoed, and her voice sounded much stronger this time.

She hugged her knees to her chest. Her hair clung to her bare arms, trailing along her skin like blood veins. I watched as she gathered it all into her hands and wrung it out, water splashing to the floor as she squeezed every last drop from her long hair. The wind snaked along my back, my soaked shirt offering no protection. Lightning flashed, and we both flinched. Laiken curled up against me. I stiffened as she leaned her head against my shoulder with a soft sigh. We stayed like that for a few long moments, and then I allowed myself to relax.

I don't know how long we sat there like that, listening to the storm outside. Laiken fell asleep at some point, curled up against my side with her arms wrapped loosely around herself. I must have dozed off myself as well, because when I blinked awake, morning had arrived and the storm was nothing more than the occasional pitter-patter of rain against the roof whenever the wind shook the water out of the trees.

The both of us were still damp. I felt sticky, my clothes

clinging to me uncomfortably. I shifted, stretching out both legs to ease the cramps that had formed. Laiken was still fast asleep.

"Laiken," I murmured, giving her a gentle shake. "Wake up."

Her eyelids fluttered open, revealing her piercing blue eyes. "Is it over?" she mumbled, her words half-slurred and nearly indecipherable.

"It's over," I confirmed.

She opened her eyes fully then, pushing herself up to see out the window. A sigh of relief blew past her lips as she sat back again. "Oh, thank the Lord."

"We're wet," I said, scowling as I peeled Laiken's wet hair off my arm, "but we're alive."

I stood up, my back popping as I stretched my arms overhead. The floor was soaked with water, a massive puddle underneath the open window that let the rain in all night long. The storm had cooled off the air considerably. Instead of the sticky heat I was used to, a chilly breeze now swept through the hallway, sending a cold shiver down my spine. It didn't help that my clothes were still wet. My boots squelched with every step I took.

"Are you okay?" I asked, helping Laiken to her feet.

"I think so." She scrubbed her face. "I'm still shaking after the incident with the mutant. It had its teeth right at my throat before I was able to kill it."

"You scared me," I said. "You were gone when I turned around, and then I heard you screaming…" I winced, rubbing the back of my neck. "I'm glad you're okay, Laiken."

Her eyes widened, and I realized I'd said something wrong.

"Aw, you care about me, don't you?" she teased.

I turned away. "All I said is that I'm glad you're alive."

"*No*, you said you're glad I'm *okay*." Laiken waltzed up to me, grinning from ear to ear. "You were scared because you thought I was hurt. You care about me, Bull."

"I cared for a minute, but now you've ruined the moment," I muttered.

Laiken let the subject drop, but I didn't miss her smirk as she studied the window.

"Any idea where we are?" she asked.

I opened the front door to get a view of the outside. My mouth fell open as I took in the damage.

"Lord a'mercy," Laiken whispered.

The tree in the front yard had been uprooted and now lay sideways across the yard. Its branches twisted this way and that, the longest ones brushing against the porch as the wind whipped them to and fro. If the wind had been blowing in just a slightly different direction, the tree would have landed right on top of the house.

Right on top of *us*.

I swallowed. "That could have been bad."

Laiken tentatively stepped towards it, running a hand over the massive trunk. That tree was big and old; I didn't even think I could get my arms around it. I was surprised we hadn't heard it fall—a rumble of thunder must have covered the sound.

Laiken glanced at me over her shoulder. "There were a bunch of trees near our hideout. If one this big was tipped over, what are the chances all of those are still standing?"

I winced as I thought of our hideout, of all the precious supplies we left there. We still had all the stuff at Laiken's church we could go back to—assuming nobody had found it and taken it for themselves—but resources were not something you just tossed out the door. If a tree had fallen on our hideout, we would need to go in and salvage whatever we could.

My gaze traveled past the overturned tree, surveying the damage. Sticks and limbs and leaves littered the ground. Puddles of water reflected the gray morning light. The street was flooded. We would have a hard time getting back to the hideout in this mess.

"Do you still have the map?" I asked.

We brought only the necessary supplies for our trip to Freeport. My pack and most of our gear were left back at the hideout, but Laiken had tucked one of her maps in her back pocket to help us navigate to the city. She pulled it out now, wincing as the wet paper disintegrated in her hands.

"I *had* the map," she muttered.

"It's okay. We're still in the general area; it can't be that hard to find."

The tree was blocking our way out. I grabbed onto one of the lower branches and used it to hoist myself up so I was standing on top of the trunk. I offered Laiken a hand up. She gave me a smile as I hauled her up next to me. For a moment, the two of us teetered at the top of the trunk, frowning at the debris on the ground. Then Laiken let out a shout and jumped down, her blue hair flying behind her. Shaking my head, I stepped down and followed her.

THIRTEEN

"Stop that!"

Laiken just gave me a look of cool contempt as she jumped into the next puddle, sending another wave of water flying towards me.

"Poor Bull," she crooned. "He doesn't like having any fun, does he?"

"You're splashing me," I muttered, wringing out my shirt for the fifth time.

Laiken waded through the ankle-deep water. The storm caused some major flooding in the outskirts of Freeport. Water covered half the street. Laiken splashed through the underwater portion while I did my best to stay dry on the opposite sidewalk.

"We're both already wet," Laiken said. "What's the harm in getting even more wet and having fun while we're at it?"

"The point," I growled, "is that I would have already been dry if not for you."

Laiken clicked her tongue and splashed me again.

I had no idea where we were. Nothing looked familiar. We'd been walking for a few hours, or so I thought—it was hard to gauge the time when the sun remained firmly behind a thick layer of gray clouds that extended from one horizon to the other. There hadn't been any more rain beyond a faint rumble of thunder that had Laiken and I bolting for cover until we were sure a fresh round of storms wasn't on the way.

There were a lot of downed trees and flooded streets, branches that blocked walkways and even a house that appeared to have collapsed during the storm. My favorite was the tree limb we found impaled through a mutant's chest in the middle of the street. Laiken's method of processing the danger we were in yesterday—we slept through the entire night—was jumping in every puddle she came across and annoying me while she did it. I told her when she looked like a child; she just stuck her tongue out at me to prove my point.

"I'm tired," she announced. "And starving."

We didn't have any food on us. The single sack of food and water we'd brought to support our trip to Freeport had been lost in the confusion of the storm. I was hungry and tired as well, but I narrowed my eyes at Laiken. "If you'd quit splashing around, you'd conserve more energy and wouldn't be as tired."

She countered, "If I quit splashing around, I wouldn't have anything to entertain myself with and would annoy you further by complaining nonstop about how hungry and tired I am."

I swept my gaze across the houses on either side of us. A tree had fallen into one, smashing it to bits. The buildings on Laiken's side of the street had water flowing through every crack and crevice. Everything was rain-soaked and ramshackle, unfit for a proper shelter and not appealing in the least.

I turned back to Laiken. "We should keep looking. I want to find our way back before nightfall."

Or before another round of storms hit, I thought, glancing at the still-gray sky.

Laiken followed my gaze with a small frown. "Okay."

We reached the end of the street. On one side were more houses and buildings and what might have been a factory of some sorts; to the other lay a stretch of woods. I exchanged a look with Laiken, who offered nothing more than a shrug before taking off into the trees.

"It's going to be muddy," I muttered. Indeed, my boots sank into the soft ground with every step.

Laiken shot me a look as she pulled her hair back into a ponytail. "Don't tell me you're afraid of getting a little dirty."

"I'm not afraid. I'm just wondering how clean I can get without a proper shower to wash all this mud off."

"You're no fun."

"We're in the wastelands, Laiken. We're here for survival, not fun."

"What's the point of surviving if you aren't enjoying it?" Laiken shrugged. "I don't just want to live; I want to enjoy the life I have." She paused, squinting through the trees. "There's a clearing up ahead. Is that—?"

Without further warning, Laiken took off, sloshing through the mud. I jogged after her. It soon became apparent what had drawn her attention—a short stretch of beach, the ocean beyond it, the waves hitting the rocks and sand with more intensity than it had the last time I'd seen it. The water was a cloudy gray, nothing more than a rolling reflection of the sky above.

Laiken put her hands on her hips and surveyed the debris-ridden beach. "Does this look familiar to you?" she asked.

"No."

"It looks kind of like the place we swam at," she said, nudging a twig with her foot. "The same kind of rocks and trees. I think we're close."

"To where we went swimming?"

My words fell on deaf ears. Laiken's head swiveled back and forth as she looked from side to side, trying to judge which way we should go. I crossed my arms and waited. Eventually, Laiken closed her eyes, took a deep breath, and pointed to the right.

"I think it's that way," she said.

I didn't move. "It's the ocean, Laiken. It all looks the same."

"You've only seen one part of the ocean before. How do you know?"

"I've seen pictures."

"And they all looked *exactly* like this beach? I don't think so."

Laiken marched off in the direction she indicated, her blue ponytail swinging with every step. Despite the fact she was soaking wet and her calves were splattered with mud, she walked with an air of importance, like she owned the entire wastelands. Laiken acted like she existed in a separate world from the rest of us. A world where there was always hope, always something to look forward to, not the bleak existence I was used to.

It was almost like she didn't realize we were living in the apocalypse. That there were flesh-eating monsters roaming around every corner. That living out here in the wastelands was a punishment, not something to be happy about.

And yet, Laiken was perhaps the most happy, charismatic person I'd ever met.

I couldn't wrap my mind around it.

I debated leaving Laiken to her exploring and going back to the street to search, but after yesterday, I couldn't bring myself to do it. I could still hear her screaming my name over the roar of the wind, panicked and desperate. She had befriended me, even if I didn't return the sentiment. If I were going to leave her and go on my own, I should have done it days ago. It seemed wrong to do it now.

So I ducked my head and trudged after Laiken.

We hadn't walked but for maybe a half an hour before Laiken stopped and spun around, flashing me a triumphant grin. She didn't have to say a word, because I could see the beach past her.

The very familiar beach.

"You found it," I said, not quite believing it. It was the same beach—the same crooked tree stretched over the water, the same cropping of rocks Laiken stood on to be as tall as I was, the same length of sand, though it was now littered with debris from the storm. I shook my head, fighting back a sigh. *Damn her.*

Laiken's grin only grew. "How do you like that, ye of little faith? I knew where I was going!"

"No, you didn't."

"You're right. I really had no idea where I was going." She gestured around. "But it worked out for the best, didn't it?"

I only motioned for her to keep walking. Now that we had our bearings, it took no time for us to clamber across the rocks and start back to our hideout. I didn't think it was possible for Laiken to smile any bigger. I glared at the back of her head as we walked, a tiny bit of me hating her.

The hideout came into view, and I let out a sigh of relief. It was a far shot from home—*home* being my apartment back in Austin I'd lived in since I was fifteen—but it still eased something in my chest to see it. It was safe; it had all our supplies, and most importantly, it had escaped being hit by a tree.

Ahead of me, I saw Laiken's shoulders slump, giving in to that similar feeling of relief.

We headed for the hideout. A flash of mute red caught my

eye.

Curiosity got the better of me, and I jogged towards it. It was the wagon full of supplies—now floating in the flooded ditch. I winced.

"I don't think we'll be able to salvage that," Laiken said, coming up behind me.

"I should have gone back for it." I grabbed a stick and poked at the wagon, sending ripples across the surface of the water. "Too late now."

Brown clouds of mud swirled as the stick scraped the bottom of the ditch. Sighing, I let it drop into the water. Laiken grimaced. "That's the least of our problems right now. Come on—I want to get into some dry clothes."

I shot her an incredulous look. "If you wanted to be dry, you shouldn't have—"

"Jumped in all the puddles," she finished, waving a flippant hand. "I know, I know. But right now I'm cold and wet and since I can't change the past, I'll change my clothes instead." She nudged me with her elbow. "Let's go."

Rolling my eyes, I walked up the street to our hideout. It was on a hill, saved from the flooding. Puddles still formed in the driveway, and I did my best to step around them, thankful to see Laiken do the same.

Despite the lack of reinforcements, the door and windows were still standing. I pushed the former open and ducked my head as I stepped in. Laiken brushed past me, already kicking off her wet sneakers as she made her way into the living room where our supplies were. I leaned against the wall to unlace my boots, but a sharp gasp from Laiken had me racing to her side.

"What—" I pulled up short as I entered the living room.

Laiken grabbed my arm. "Our stuff is gone."

Indeed it was. I fought back a curse as I surveyed the

ransacked living room, all of Laiken's careful cleaning completely undone. My pack and my rifle were both gone. Laiken's stuff was gone as well. But what angered me the most was the message on the far wall, scrawled in red spray paint:

THE VIPERS WERE HERE.

FOURTEEN

"The Vipers," Laiken breathed. "I thought they left."

"We both did." I stepped towards the message on the wall, studying the paint.

"We haven't even been gone a full day! How did they make it back so quickly?"

I swiped a finger across the V, frowning as it smeared. "I don't think they ever left. They were hiding somewhere." I rubbed the paint between two fingers. It looked like blood. "And they're still not gone. This paint is fresh."

Laiken went stiff. "They're still here?"

"They're close. Stay here."

I drew my gun and darted for the back door. The door handle was broken, keeping it from shutting all the way, so Laiken had tied a rope between the handle and a nearby table to keep it pulled shut. The rope was still in place, which meant the Vipers hadn't entered through there.

And they hadn't exited there, either.

The paint was still dripping in some spots. It was fresh, done only a few minutes ago. Laiken and I had a view of the front of this house for over ten minutes during our walk up the street. We hadn't seen anyone coming or going through the front door. And if the Vipers hadn't gone through the back...

I returned to Laiken's side and whispered, "They're in this building somewhere."

Every muscle in her body went rigid as she finished pulling her shoes back on. "Where?"

"I don't know," I breathed. "Stay close and don't say a word."

I edged into the kitchen and then peered into the hallway beyond. This house had a second floor, but the stairs were rotten and Laiken had blocked them off with another length of rope tied between the two rails. I didn't think anyone would be up there. I moved through the lower rooms like a wraith, my steps silent.

I ran over the situation in my mind as I opened the door to a bedroom and found no one inside.

One Viper might have seen us leaving for Freeport, giving them free rein to search for us. Nico tracked us to this house.

Laiken drew in a breath as I opened another door and was greeted by nothing but an empty room.

The storm would have struck while they were searching the house. They took shelter here for the night, then in the morning, decided to make use of our wide variety of supplies.

Nobody was in the bathroom or the broom closet.

They lingered longer than they meant to—or maybe they assumed we perished in the storm and would never come back. So they stayed as long as they liked. At some point, somebody thought it would be a good idea to move, so they packed up our gear and spray-painted a message on the wall just in case we made it back alive.

There was only one door left to check. The one Laiken thought led to the basement.

The Vipers meant to clear out—but they heard or saw us approach before they could make it, forcing them to hide in the house itself.

Or more specifically, in the basement.

Laiken reached for the door handle, but I drew her back, silently herding her back into the living room.

"They aren't here," I called, making sure my voice seemed loud and angry, annoyed by this whole situation. "Come on, Laiken, we should search outside."

Laiken looked confused. "You think they left already?"

"They probably headed down the street through the back door." I kept my voice loud—loud enough to be heard in the basement. "Maybe we can catch up to them."

I grabbed Laiken's arm and stomped to the front door. I opened it, then slammed it without walking out. Laiken was looking at me like I had three heads, but I ignored her as I quietly pulled her into the first bedroom.

"Bull, what are you doing?" she hissed.

"Quiet," I murmured. "They're in the basement, I think. We're luring them out."

Just strolling down into the basement would have been a bad idea. The Vipers had my rifle on top of their own weapons—they would shoot us before we made it to the third stair. So Laiken and I waited in tense silence. We sat there for so long I became convinced I was wrong and that the Vipers weren't here at all. I even started to stand up and tell Laiken we were in the clear, but then I heard the distinctive sound of a door opening.

Accompanied by the quiet murmur of voices.

Laiken went wholly still beside me as Nico's voice floated to us.

"Give me the gun, asshole. We should have already killed them!"

"No," a nasally voice—perhaps Josh with his broken nose—said. "They think we're gone, so we should—"

"I don't care about what we should or shouldn't do," Nico

snapped.

The third guy chimed in, "Guys, we really should get out of here. They might come back."

Nico and Josh ignored them as they continued their argument. I eased open the door, giving myself a sliver of a view. Nico stood further down the hallway, Josh in front of him, the two of them nose-to-nose and arguing over the gun like children fighting over a toy. The third Viper nervously shifted his feet, shooting glances to the front door.

"Guys," he interjected again, "we need to get out of here. Now."

Nico snarled at him. "Shut your mouth, Ren."

"Boss—"

"*I said shut up!*"

"They could come back at any minute," Ren snapped.

"Scared to face the giant?" he sneered.

"Anyone in their right mind would!"

A bitter sense of satisfaction rippled through me at that.

Josh stepped between the two of them, still holding my rifle. "Ren's right, boss. We need to leave." He winced. "And it wouldn't hurt to keep our voices down."

"When did you get righteous?" Nico snarked, but he did lower his voice, just a touch. He grabbed the rifle from Josh, who let out a cry of protest. Nico ignored him and stalked for the front door. He made it far enough to put his hand on the door before Josh grabbed him from behind.

Laiken and I jerked back as the two began scuffling right in front of the door we hid behind.

"Keep your filthy hands off of me," Nico snarled, his black eyes wild with fury.

"Give me the gun," Josh countered, giving him a shove.

"Asshole—"

"Filthy rat—"

"Stop—"

"Give it to me—"

"Get off—"

"Quit it, the both of you," Ren hissed. He thrummed with anxiety, casting nervous glances through the windows, as if expecting me to come barreling through at any time. I braced myself as Josh slammed Nico into the wall—causing the rifle to fly out of his hands. Josh tried to grab it; Nico hauled him back by the neck of his shirt and punched him in the jaw. With a feral snarl, he threw himself back into the fight, the gun forgotten for the moment.

I exchanged a look with Laiken before wrenching open the door and pressing my pistol against Nico's temple in one smooth motion.

Josh scrambled back, stunned at my sudden appearance. Ren muttered something that sounded like a prayer. Nico scrambled for a weapon, but I wrapped one arm around his throat and dragged him back, my gun digging into the side of his head. There was a flash of blue as Laiken darted out of her hiding spot, scooped up the fallen rifle, and scrambled to my side.

It was with no small amount of satisfaction that I noted how pale the Vipers' faces had gotten.

"Move," I said to Nico, my voice dangerously low, "and I'll pull the trigger."

He went still. Very, very still.

I turned to the other two. "Either of you move, and my friend will be the one to pull the trigger."

Laiken hefted the rifle onto her shoulder and swept it between them.

Ren was shaking. "How—You left—"

I didn't feel like explaining it to him, so I didn't bother. "Laiken and I have done nothing to upset you. You three thought she was alone and tried to rob her, and when I stopped you from doing so, you tracked us down and tried to rob the both of us." I dug the gun harder into Nico's temple. "I told you three to *get lost*. And what did you do? You tracked us *again* and tried to take our stuff."

"Not cool," Laiken chimed in.

Nico sneered. I couldn't see his face from my position, but that was probably a good thing for him—I would be very tempted to punch him the next time I saw his annoying little sneer.

"I'm going to kill you," he said.

I leaned down so my mouth was near his ear.

"Try that," I whispered, "and I will *slaughter* you."

He had the good sense to close his damn mouth after that.

I raised my head to glare at Ren and Josh. "Drop your stuff," I commanded. *Our* stuff, mostly. When they didn't move, I said, louder, "*Drop it. All of it. Now.*"

Laiken raised the rifle in warning. "Do what he says, or we'll kill you."

I scowled. My plan had been to kill them regardless—I wanted them to drop the supplies so I didn't catch any of it with a stray bullet and destroy something useful. Laiken hadn't known that, but a small part of me found myself desperately wishing the Vipers would refuse, just to give me a reason to shoot them all where they stood.

But Ren instantly shrugged off the pack he was wearing. *My* pack, I noted with fury. After a brief hesitation, Josh dropped his stuff too, even going as far as to remove the belt that held up his gun holster.

I gave Nico a little shove. "Now you."

With deliberate slowness, he dropped his bags to the ground. His pistol followed a moment later.

Laiken waved the rifle at the other two. "Back up." They did so without question, and Laiken darted forwards to collect our things. The Vipers had dropped all their belongings, the stuff they had previously alongside the gear they stole from us. I didn't feel bad about taking theirs. They deserved every bit of this.

They deserved more than this, if you asked me. It was taking every bit of self control I possessed not to pull the trigger and send Nico De La Cruz to his grave.

I gripped Nico's shoulder hard enough to leave a bruise. "I want you to listen to me very carefully," I said. "This is the third time you've tried to screw with us. And it's the third time you've had your asses handed to you. One would think that you've learned your lesson by now, but since you seem like the kind of stubborn ass to come back and try again, I'm going to make sure I get my point across loud and clear." I lowered my voice. "If I ever see you or one of your Vipers ever again… If I hear about you or see where you've painted your name somewhere… If I even get the slightest feeling that you're try-ing to hunt us down again…" I bared my teeth. "I will personally hunt each and every one of you down and teach you what real pain feels like. This"—I pressed down on his shoulder even harder—"is *nothing* compared to what I can do to you. And hopefully you get all of this through your thick skull before I bash it into your brains. Understand?"

Nico was trembling. Whether he was shaking out of fury or fear, I didn't know. "I understand," he said, and his voice was tight. Restrained. Full of loathing.

He was definitely furious.

The thought pleased me.

"Good," I said, shoving him forward. It was hard enough to send him careening face-first into the door. He hit it with a grunt, and when he faced me again, his eyes glinting with barely concealed anger, blood dripped from his nose and lips. I waved impatiently. "Get out of here."

Nico opened his mouth—to say what, I didn't know—but Ren grabbed his arm. His eyes were wide as he hauled Nico out the door. Josh was on his other side, helping to pull their leader out before he started a fight he wouldn't be able to finish.

It was only after they left, after I watched them trek down the street through the window, did I realize I was trembling with fury. I hadn't felt this angry since my first few weeks in prison, and that thought alone subdued me.

"We should leave."

I turned towards Laiken. She gingerly held out my rifle to me as she repeated, "We should leave. Now. Before they come back."

I studied her. We were both still wet and cold and hungry and exhausted. We needed to rest, to change into fresh clothes and to eat, to sort through our supplies and figure out a plan.

"We need to stay here for tonight," I said at last.

"But what if the Vipers come back?"

"They won't." Not if they had any sense.

"But what if they do?" Laiken pressed.

My hands curled into fists. "I'll keep watch while you rest, and we'll leave first thing in the morning. If they try to attack, it won't be before then. They have no supplies, no weapons. We took it all. They'll probably head back to wherever their base is, stock up, then come back to find us—and by then, we'll be long gone."

Laiken's throat bobbed. "Are you sure?"

"Positive."

This didn't seem to reassure her much, but she nodded all the same. I turned back to the window, my jaw clenched.

I still should have killed them, I thought, not for the first time. But it was too late now.

FIFTEEN

The first order of business was to dry off.

Laiken changed her clothes while I kept watch at the window. When she returned in a fresh tank top and leggings, her unbound hair spilling over her shoulders, I ducked into the bedroom and stripped off every article of wet clothing. I dug a fresh set out of my pack and pulled them on with a sigh of relief. My boots would take a while to dry. I wanted to be prepared to leave at a moment's notice—which meant staying fully dressed, shoes and all—but I resigned to leaving them by the door in an effort to dry them out by morning.

Laiken was well into her way of taking care of the second order of business—eating—by the time I sat down next to her, feeling much better now that I was dry. Her sketchbook was in her lap, though it wasn't open. She silently handed me a can of soup and a spoon.

And she didn't speak for the rest of the night.

I assumed it was worry keeping her quiet, but at some point in the dead of night, long after Laiken had fallen asleep and I was keeping watch by the window, I began to wonder if she was mad at me for not allowing us to leave right away. It would have been the smart thing to do if not for the state we were both in.

My mind drifted to last night, when Laiken had fallen asleep next to me. I kept seeing her face, serene in sleep, the corners of her mouth tilted up in the hint of a smile. Peaceful, despite the storm that raged outside.

I liked her being next to me like that, and the thought made me uncomfortable.

A soft scratching sound had me bolting upright. I listened in the dark, my head tilted to the side, my fingers curling around my rifle. It sounded again, and then I was in motion.

Quietly, I stepped over Laiken's sleeping form and headed for that noise. I tensed as it came again. A soft *scraaatch* from the back of the house.

I reached the back door and gave the rope a tug to make sure it was tight. It was perfectly intact. None of the windows back here opened; I verified that for myself upon first entering this house. The only way to get through back here was to break the windows, which I would hear, or to cut the rope from the outside.

Satisfied, I turned to go back to my post, but the same noise had me whirling with my finger on the trigger of my gun. My eyes landed on the source: a tree branch, rubbing against the windows as the wind caused it to dance back and forth.

My shoulders relaxed. Nothing was out of the ordinary.

I returned to my silent vigil by the window. I sat on the windowsill, my legs tucked underneath me, my rifle resting in my lap. Laiken hadn't moved at all, the rise and fall of her chest the only sign she was still alive. The moon peeked through the clouds, offering small rays of silver light to see by. I swept my gaze over the street, confirming for the hundredth time that it remained empty and quiet.

Nothing out of the ordinary, I thought, fighting back a yawn.

I was tired. Exhausted, even. But I stayed awake until the crack of dawn, until the first few rays of sunlight graced the sky.

Blankets rustled, and I glanced over to see Laiken sitting up, blinking at me with bleary eyes.

"You're still awake?" she asked. "You should have let me keep watch part of the time."

I shrugged as I unfolded my legs and stretched them out. "You needed rest."

"I'm not the only one."

"I'm fine," I said, rising to my feet. It was light enough outside to see by. We needed to get going. I told Laiken that, cutting her off before she could say anything else.

We had unpacked very little the night before, so it took no time at all to get everything ready to travel. I tugged on my boots, wincing as I realized they were still damp on the inside. Laiken insisted we eat before we left.

"I was thinking we should head back to your church," I said over breakfast.

Laiken blinked. "But wouldn't we have to walk right through where we first met the Vipers? That seems counter-productive."

"Can't we swing around the long way and avoid that place?" I crumpled up my trash and threw it aside, scowling as I recalled the dingy playground where we had first encountered Nico and his entourage. "You know this area better than I do."

"I don't know it *that* well."

I thought back to how Laiken found her way back here yesterday and decided she was underestimating her navigational abilities.

"What *are* we going to do about the Vipers?" Laiken asked. "I mean, they might try to follow us. We haven't eliminated the threat."

"That," I said, "is something we will worry about when the time comes."

We left soon after that. The path we took from the ocean back to the church had seen its fair share of damage. We encountered a fallen tree almost immediately—judging by the way the bark was charred and blackened, I suspected it had been hit by lightning. The further we went, the fewer debris we came across, and by the time we stopped to rest for the night, there were barely any signs a storm came through save for the occasional puddle. Which Laiken always stopped to splash around in.

I remained silent for most of the walk. Laiken offered up a steady stream of conversation to fill the silence, always careful to never mention the Vipers or what had occurred yesterday. She told me a lot of stories about her childhood, running around Houston with her older sister, Lucy. Or that's the parts I heard, at least—I tuned out most of her words in favor of my own thoughts.

I thought she forgot about the Vipers for the time being, but as soon as we settled down in the old shed we found for that night's shelter, she propped her chin up with one hand and asked, "So, what are we going to do about the Vipers?"

I was *exhausted*. I'd had nothing but adrenaline rush after adrenaline rush since the storm hit, and I hadn't had a proper sleep since then. Laiken might be well-rested enough to chatter on for days, but I was in no mood to talk.

"If they come back," I said flatly, "I'll kill them."

Laiken sucked on her teeth. "Just like that?"

"Just like that," I agreed. "Now go to sleep."

"Aren't we going to keep watch?"

"*I'm* going to keep watch while *you* sleep."

"I'll take the first watch," Laiken announced, setting aside her sketchbook, which she'd been doodling in for the past few minutes. "Since you didn't sleep last night. You've been moodier than usual today, so I know you have to be tired."

I narrowed my eyes on her. "I'll keep watch."

As tired as I was, the only person I trusted to keep a proper eye out for Nico was myself. The only way to make sure something gets done right, Slater always said, was to do it yourself. No delegating tasks, no trusting others to get the dirty work done. You just rolled up your sleeves and did it.

My last assignment as Slater's assassin, I'd been forced to work with another agent. An agent who turned me in not a week later. We'd never gotten along; while he claimed he had turned me over because he was scared of our assigned target, because he felt it was the *right thing to do* at that moment, I highly suspected he had just done it out of spite. I had never been one to work well with people before that, but while sitting in my prison cell, I told myself that if I ever got out, I'd inform Slater I wouldn't be going on joint missions ever again.

And I wasn't about to break that vow now.

"I'll keep watch," I said again.

"You'll fall asleep," Laiken retorted.

I snorted. "That's what you think. I've been doing this for years; I know how to keep my eyes open." I looked her up and down. "Unlike others."

"Oh, come on, Bull. This isn't rocket science. I know how to stand by a window with a gun and shoot anything that moves."

"That is *not*—"

"It most certainly is!"

"You're not qualified," I snapped. "You—"

"Qualified?" Laiken repeated, arching a brow. "What is that supposed to mean? Lord a'mercy, Bull, if anyone is qualified to stand watch for the night, it's me. I'm the one who's been out here for two years already. You're not the king of the wastelands."

I was primed to continue that argument, but her words made me pause. "Two years?"

"That's what I said," she affirmed with a small nod. "Here by choice."

I sat down, studying Laiken over the remains of the small fire we'd constructed in the shed. It probably hadn't been the wisest choice, starting a fire in the middle of an ancient shed made of very flammable wood, but we hadn't wanted the light attracting mutants.

"Why?" I asked quietly. "Why did you leave?"

What could have possibly been so bad to make you so happy while living out in the wastelands?

Laiken picked at the hem of her shirt. "When I was in Houston," she said, not quite meeting my gaze, "most people didn't like me. And I get it—it's a bad world out there, and not everyone appreciates my optimistic BS. My sister is the only one who liked it. My parents sure didn't. I don't mean to annoy people. It's just natural to me, to look for reasons to be happy. I don't get the point of going through life upset. If you're alive, then you have a reason to be thankful, right?

"Well, I bugged people. I was that annoying kid nobody liked. Which I hated, because I am a people person." She smiled at me. "You've probably figured that out."

I grunted my agreement.

Laiken chuckled, but her smile didn't last long. "My parents had a friend who had a son about my age. His name was Avery. The family was respected, and he showed an interest in me, so my parents pushed me to date him. They thought he would... calm me down. I never liked him, and neither did Lucy—my sister. But my parents wanted me to, and I wanted someone to like me, so we got together. And it was alright, at first. Avery was nice most of the time, but when he wanted something or when he was angry… he became mean. Cruel. Unapproachable. I hated that about him."

She shivered. "We dated for a year. Then one of Avery's friends got into it with him. About what, I don't know, but one day they got drunk and had a huge argument. They weren't thinking straight, so I pulled Avery aside to tell him so. But he was drunk and livid. He slapped me across the face before I could get a word out. I was stunned, to say the least—nobody had ever laid a hand on me like that before. So I ran home, crying and upset, and hid in my room for hours.

"I wanted to tell someone, but everyone regarded Avery as the golden boy—government worker, wealthy family, highly respected… He could do no wrong, in their view." Laiken stared at the weak flames. "Avery sobered up that night and came to find me. I expected an apology. Remorse. Anything. But he started lecturing me about what I did. He pretended the slap never happened. I was so done with him at that point, so fed up, that I gave it right back to him. We argued for over an hour, screaming at each other loud enough the neighbors threatened to call the authorities. I told Avery that we were done and he should leave. He refused, so I tried to shove him out the door.

"And that's when he pulled a knife on me."

SIXTEEN

A tear slipped down Laiken's cheek, and I realized it was the first time I'd ever seen her cry.

"Avery stabbed me," Laiken said, her voice distant and hollow. She pulled up her shirt a bit, tracing one finger over a faint scar on her abdomen. "He saw what he'd done and took off; I ran to Lucy for help. She patched me up and went straight to the guard post to tell them what Avery had done to me. But when she got there, she heard him telling the soldiers that a mutant had somehow gotten into the compound and bitten me."

A cold sense of dread settled deep in my stomach. I knew what that meant. Mutants were not allowed within Safe Zone walls—and neither was anyone who'd been bitten by one, even if they hadn't fully transformed yet. Anyone with a bite inside the Zones was to be put down immediately and without question.

"Smart move on his part," I murmured. A horrible thing to do, but a smart way to cover up his tracks. I tucked that information aside.

Laiken's voice shook. "Lucy ran back to me and told me I had to get out of the city immediately. I was scared and confused, but I trusted her more than anyone, so I did what she said. She packed me a bag and helped me get past the gate. She told me to wait for a couple of weeks, more than long enough to prove that I hadn't been bitten and was perfectly healthy, then to go to a different Safe Zone and write her a letter from there. She didn't want me anywhere near Avery ever again.

"So I made it to the wastelands and ran. I never looked back. After about three weeks, I think, I stumbled across the man who used to live in the church. We saw each other from afar a few times but never talked. He was legitimately crazy. Then one day, I saw him get attacked by mutants. They bit him. I tried to help him, but it was too late. He told me to go to the church before he shot himself in the head to keep from transforming." She shrugged, angrily wiping away her tears. "I never saw a reason to go back. I was too afraid of Avery finding me, of him doing something to Lucy if he found out how she had helped me. I was too damn scared. So I never made it back to a Safe Zone, never wrote Lucy that letter I promised. She probably thinks I'm dead."

"Avery," I muttered, "sounds like an asshole."

A laugh cracked out of Laiken. "The greatest asshole to ever walk the earth," she agreed, and I was glad to see that some of the spark had returned to her eyes. "But that's why I'm out here. Because of him. Because of my parents, for forcing me to be with him. Because of everyone else in that stupid town that thought he was a good person."

"I'd kill him for you if I ever got the chance," I said.

Laiken snorted. "That's what every girl wants to hear, isn't it?"

"I mean it."

"I'm sure you do." She swiped at her face again, clearing away the last of the tears. "What about you, Bull? I know you're not out here just to kill mutants. There's more to it than that."

I lifted one shoulder in a shrug. "I lived in Austin. My parents died when I was eight, and President Slater took me in."

"*The* President Slater?"

"The very one. He was the VP then. He thought he saw potential in me, so he trained me to fight. To kill. I did his dirty work for years—and I was good at it."

She hugged her knee to her chest. "So what went wrong? Why are you here?"

I stared at the fire. "I was put on a joint mission with another agent. Neither of us were the type to work well with others, and we certainly did not get along. There was a group of dissenters in the Denver Safe Zone that Slater wanted killed. I got into a fight with the other agent over who should take lead on the mission. He got pissed off and went to the dissenters to tell them about me. I killed the dissenters but not before they alerted the authorities. I was arrested when I got back to Austin. The Council intervened and took over for the Denver authorities. Slater had always promised me that if I were caught, he would pardon me for my actions since I'd only been doing his work for the beginning. I pleaded guilty at my trial thinking that I would get my pardon, but pardons have to be approved by the Council, and they didn't approve of mine, so I was put up for execution."

Laiken blinked. "Did the Council know you worked for Slater?"

"They did."

"So why didn't they—"

"The Council didn't want the public knowing that I worked with the government. It was common knowledge that I was basically Slater's adopted kid, so rumors were already flying that I worked for him. If I were pardoned, then in the public's eye, it was proof that I was an assassin." I raked a hand through my hair. "If I were punished instead, it made it seem like I was just a killer who had no backing from the government. The Council was hellbent on killing me to make sure I didn't let the truth slip. So they put me up for execution and let the public declare me a serial killer. The agent who turned me in was given a nice compensation to keep his mouth shut. Slater managed to talk the Council into exile instead." I gestured around. "And here I am."

There was a beat of silence. Then Laiken said, her voice wry, "I see you're still keeping up with that I'm-a-serial-killer storyline, hmm?"

I blinked at her. "It's the truth."

Laiken shrugged. Mischief danced in her eyes, replacing the hollow sadness from when she'd been telling her story. "I just find it hard to believe."

"Do you think I just made all of that up?"

"You've had days to think up a story," she countered.

I groaned at the roof. "I'm telling the truth."

Laiken gave me a knowing smile. "Sure you are."

I shook my head, a smile curling over my lips.

Laiken gasped. "What's wrong with your face? That couldn't be a smile, could it? Is it possible for the brooding assassin to crack a smile?"

I struggled to replace my small grin with a scowl. "I don't know what you're talking about."

"He's *smiling*," Laiken sang, her eyes glinting with wicked amusement. She brushed her hands off. "I finally did it. I accomplished my life's goal of making you smile. My work here is complete, so you're on your own now."

"You're impossible," I muttered. I was truly smiling now, albeit reluctantly.

"He's smiling, he's smiling, he's *smiling*," she taunted, poking my arm with each word.

I batted her hand away, finally able to rid myself of the grin and replace it with my usual scowl. "I'll let you have first watch if you quit bugging me like this."

With a satisfied grin, Laiken grabbed my rifle and took up a spot next to the door. I rolled my eyes at her as I laid back, tucking my arms underneath my head.

"Is it really the truth?" Laiken asked a few minutes later.

I shot her a wry look. "No, I've been making it up this entire time. You've caught me."

She lifted one shoulder in a half shrug. "I am just trying to pick on you some, but at the same time, I find it hard to believe that *you* were an assassin."

"What makes you say that?"

Another shrug. "I dunno. You just don't seem like the type." She dropped a wink in my direction. "It's that heart of gold I told you about. You're too sweet to be a killer."

I choked as I propped myself up on one elbow. "I was convicted on thirty-seven counts of murder!"

"You pleaded guilty," she corrected. "Which means they didn't actually prove anything."

I crossed my arms. "So you believe that part of the story and not the rest?"

She simply shrugged for a third time and asked, "Thirty-seven?"

"That's the ones they thought they could prove in court."

She blinked. "So there were more?"

I dropped my gaze. "Yeah."

I heard Laiken shifting the rifle between her hands, breaking the weighted silence that had fallen over us. "How many were there?" she asked, her tone quiet.

"One hundred and fifty-three," I breathed.

Going on two hundred people that Slater had sent me to kill. I counted their deaths as religiously as I now counted the mutants. Most of my missions were taking out political opponents and rebel organizations, those trying to undermine the post-Virus government systems. Most of the time, I was tasked with taking out entire groups at a time.

153. Three digits. And I could recall nearly every face, every kill.

They still haunted my dreams.

I glanced up to see Laiken staring at me, her brows knit together and her eyes narrowed. She caught my gaze and cocked her head to the side.

"I still don't believe you," she said brightly.

"Why not?" I demanded. I couldn't really tell if she was just messing with me or if she genuinely didn't believe me. Damn, she could be really annoying if she wanted to be.

Laiken just gave me an annoying little smile in response and turned back to the door to keep watch. I rolled my eyes with a sigh and laid down again, folding my arms over my chest.

A quiet silence fell over the shed. The fire went out, leaving only a handful of embers behind. An hour slipped by, long enough that Laiken must have thought I was asleep, because I heard her whisper into the dark, "I believe you."

And I was glad for the darkness that hid my answering smile.

SEVENTEEN

Laiken never did wake me up to take over for watch, so I got a full night's sleep come dawn. We decided to stretch out the remaining two days of our journey into three, taking a lengthy route through a nearby city to avoid going anywhere near the playground where we first met the Vipers. We also tried to keep out of the wooded areas, where our footprints would be easier to see even to an untrained eye.

We walked for hours under the sweltering sun. My hair, slick with sweat, clung to my forehead and the back of my neck. Laiken didn't seem much better where she walked a few paces in front of me. Staying out of the woods meant sticking to the roads, where the dark asphalt made the air warmer than normal.

"Let's take a break," I panted.

Laiken leaned against the nearest tree without complaint.

"Usually I like Texas," she said, winded, tugging a water bottle out of her backpack. "Pretty landscapes. Big houses with lots of guns and supplies and such. The people here had it made before the Virus." She sipped her water. "But the heat is quite literally going to kill me."

I took a swig of my own drink. "Too bad mutants don't get heat stroke."

She snorted. "That really is a shame."

I drank some more water, pouring some over my head to

cool myself off—but just a little, because clean water was a precious resource, especially in this kind of heat. Laiken pulled out the map and studied it.

"It looks like there's a town coming up soon," she said. I watched her trace her finger along the page. "Maybe we should try to get there by nightfall?"

I scrubbed my face. "Sure."

It took a few more hours to get there. I had never been happier to see the sun setting as we walked down main street in what had once been a nice neighborhood. I broke down the door of the first house with a roof that was still intact and the two of us trudged inside, sweaty and exhausted.

Laiken let out a low whistle as she took in the hallway. "I don't think this place has been touched."

Most houses had been touched by the apocalypse at some point or another. Maybe looters broke in and gathered what they needed; or the weather slowly caused the roof to cave in, exposing the inside to the elements; or the door was left open and mutants tore up furniture and walls as they crashed through the house. This house in particular seemed like it had been left for thirty years. A thick layer of dust covered the furniture and television. A book lay face-down on the coffee table, a mug resting beside it. Picture frames still adorned the walls.

Laiken grabbed one of the pictures and squinted at it, trying to make out the faces underneath the layer of dust and cobwebs. "Looks like a couple lived here, maybe. It's hard to see."

I pulled a bandana out of my pocket and handed it to her. She scrubbed at the glass, clearing off the dust. The smiling faces of two people greeted us, a woman in a white wedding dress with golden blonde hair and a man in a tux whose dark hair was combed neatly to the side.

A ghost of a smile flitted over Laiken's face. "This kind of thing makes me happy to see. A husband and wife, happy and content. Not knowing what was coming later." She hung the picture back up. "I like to imagine where these people are now. Maybe they're in a Safe Zone, living out the last of their days."

I thought back to the pictures Laiken kept in the church. I'd never taken the time to look at them closely, but this wedding picture seemed like the kind that she would have brought back to be part of her museum.

I put a hand on her shoulder. "Come on. Let's get cleaned up."

She shrugged off her backpack as we ventured deeper into the house. There were no footprints visible in the grime on the floor; if anyone had been in here, it hadn't been anytime recently. I left Laiken to explore the bedrooms down the hall while I did a sweep of the kitchen and den.

Laiken was right when she said this place appeared untouched. There was still food in the kitchen, though everything was long past expiration and worn away by insects and mice. All the dishes in the cabinets were intact. I tried the faucet and was unsurprised when nothing came out.

I moved downstairs to the den after that. It was clear of mutants as well. I stepped around an age-old recliner on my way to the door in the back.

It took a few tries to open the heavy door. I was met with a rush of cool, dust-filled air that had me sneezing. I swept my flashlight back and forth, whistling softly as I took in the racks of glass bottles.

A wine cellar. It would be a miracle if any of it was still good. I kicked the door shut and was turning back to head upstairs when a shout split the air.

"Bull?"

I whirled towards the sound of Laiken's voice, high with panic. I was running in an instant, taking the stairs three and four at a time. Laiken stood in the doorway of the master bedroom, her eyes wide, one hand pressed against her mouth. I reached her side, angling myself in front of her as I took in the room.

Two skeletons laid on the king-sized bed. Their backs were propped up against the headboard, the gritty remnants of clothes clinging to the age-old bones. Their skulls were cracked and misshapen.

And each had a gun in their hand.

Laiken made a small, choked sound and buried her face into my chest. I wrapped an arm around her.

"It's okay," I murmured. "This happened a long time ago."

"It's the couple from the picture, isn't it?" she whispered.

I glanced at the bed again. The two corpses held each other with their spare hands, their skeletal fingers entwined even in death. They weren't living out their final days in the haven of the Safe Zones. They were here—and had been for a long time.

A double suicide to escape the wastelands. It wasn't the first I'd seen.

I brushed Laiken's hair behind her ear. "Yeah. It's the couple from the picture." I closed the door. "Let's get out of here."

She sniffed, wiping at her eyes. "No, it's getting dark and we need shelter."

"There's more houses down the street. Come on."

This time, she didn't protest. I led her outside, leaving her on the street as I searched through the house next door. Only once I confirmed there weren't any corpses lying about did I allow Laiken to come in.

I caught her in my arms before she made it all the way through the door. "Hey," I murmured. "It's okay. That was just part of being in the wastelands."

"I know," she whispered.

My arms tightened around her. "Are you hungry?"

She shook her head, and I couldn't blame her for it.

I glanced around, my eyes landing on a sad-looking armchair in the living room. "Sit here," I said, leading her to it. "I'll be right back."

Her head jerked up. "Where are you going?"

"Not far. I'll be right back."

I jogged outside before she could question it. I went back to the house next door, doing my best to not look in the direction of the master bedroom as I trotted downstairs. The door to the wine cellar creaked when I shoved it open.

I wasn't a big drinker. Sometimes after a hard mission Slater would pour me a shot of whiskey to take the edge off. That's what I searched for now, the flashlight beam casting the shadows of the various bottles of spirits onto the back wall before I found the whiskey.

The bottle in front was half-empty. I pushed it aside in favor of a fresh one, unscrewing the lid and taking an experimental sip to ensure it was good. It didn't taste great, but it seemed to still be in good condition.

It took a minute for me to track down two glasses in the kitchen. I cleaned them off using my bandana and as much water as I could spare. Satisfied with my work, I tucked the whiskey bottle under my arm and headed back to Laiken.

She raised both brows as I walked in. "I don't drink."

The bottle thumped on the rickety coffee table, barely standing after all these years. "It's never too late to start."

Laiken watched as I poured a tiny bit of whiskey into both glasses and slid one across the table to her.

"Drink up," I said.

She lifted it to her lips and took the tiniest of sips before making a face. "That's disgusting. People drink this stuff for fun?"

"It's about the feeling, not the taste." I unceremoniously knocked mine back. "And it's a feeling you could really use right now."

She took another sip, grimaced, then drank the rest in one go. "No more," she choked out, setting the glass down. "I've never been drunk and I don't intend to start now."

"Good thing that wasn't the plan," I said. I screwed the lid back on the bottle and tucked it away in my pack. "Neither of us would be any count in that condition, and the last thing I want is to be fighting the Vipers with a hangover."

A smile curled over her lips. "That would be an interesting fight."

"I know. It would almost be fair for them."

Laiken laughed then. It was quiet and reserved, but it was a genuine laugh, and I sighed in relief upon seeing Laiken back in her usual good spirit.

"I'm tired." I offered Laiken a hand up. "Ready to get some rest?"

"Oh, absolutely," she said. "Here's to hoping this house has running water so we can take a proper shower."

I snorted. I hadn't had a proper shower since I left Austin—some of the houses out here relied on wells on the property and had running water, but it was room temperature at best. If I ever got a chance to go back into the Safe Zones, the first order of business would be to take a hot shower.

"The house next door didn't have water, but we might get

lucky," I said.

Laiken sighed. "Can't hurt to wish."

"Yeah," I echoed. "It can't hurt."

EIGHTEEN

I kept watch again that night, studying Laiken where she slept on the floor, burrowed in her sleeping bag with her back facing me. She'd remained uncharacteristically quiet for the remainder of the night, curled up in the chair with her sketchbook, her brow furrowed as her pencil danced across the page. I found myself watching her more than usual. A few times she'd caught my gaze and flashed me a small smile. It sent my heart racing every time, forcing me to look away.

We made good time for the rest of our journey, leaving out first thing in the morning. There hadn't been even a whisper of the Vipers when we reached the church early in the evening the following day. I was pleased to see that it appeared untouched; Laiken's defenses had done their job. She unlocked the back door and headed straight for the supply room to ensure everything was in place. I entered the main hall and carefully picked my way between the shelves of Laiken's museum, not wanting to knock anything over.

"I need to clean up," Laiken said, trailing after me. She frowned at a vase of flowers that had withered during our time away. Her usual charisma was back in full force, the incident from a few days ago all but forgotten. "But it's about to get dark, so I guess I'll wait until tomorrow."

I dropped my pack on the ground. "That's probably a good idea."

She glanced at me. "We should do something fun."

I snorted. "Like what?"

"Like a game!"

"A game?" I echoed. "Come on, Laiken."

"What? I'm bored. And you always have this expression of complete and utter boredom at the world around you, so I figure you could use something to cheer you up." She poked my arm. "Please, Bull? It'll be fun."

I knew that look. It meant nothing but trouble.

"Fine," I muttered.

A wide grin split Laiken's face nearly in two. "There's this game my sister and I used to play that is so much fun. You will love it." I raised a brow and she amended, "You will somewhat enjoy yourself, at least." She brandished her sketchbook. "Come on, I'll show you what it is. Unless you want to eat first?"

"I'm good," I said, curiosity getting the better of me.

Laiken sauntered over to the pulpit and took a seat on the stage behind it, sitting cross-legged on the floor. I joined her. She flipped to the back of her book and ripped out a couple of pages, then proceeded to rip those pages into smaller rectangles.

"My sister and I played this game all the time," she explained, stacking the paper rectangles on the ground next to her. "We invented it. It's called Dare, because we couldn't think of a better name. It's super simple. Each of us will get a set of dice. We'll both roll and biggest number wins, best two out of three. The loser of each round has to draw a card"—she gestured to her sheets of paper—"and do whatever is written on it."

"A dare," I filled in.

"That's the name of the game," she agreed. "Hang on—I'll

go get some dice."

She bounded away to the back room. Her sketchbook was still on the ground. After a quick glance over my shoulder to make sure she was gone, I flipped it open to a random page and examined it. There wasn't anything special about it; it was a page of random sketches and doodles in various colors. There was a flower and a thick tangle of vines in one corner, a swirl of blue that appeared to be a river, a bird in flight, a dark thundercloud, and even a rudimentary drawing of two stick figures, one with flowing hair, the other outrageously tall and supporting a pair of bull horns.

I snorted softly and flipped the page. My hand stilled as I beheld the drawing that covered the next page.

It was a portrait of me, done in pencil, a slight smile curling over my lips.

I heard Laiken's footsteps and quickly snapped the book shut.

She sat down again and handed me two dice and a marker. "You can write whatever dares you want, as long as we have the material and time to do them," she said, also passing over a stack of paper cards. "They'll be mixed at random, so keep in mind that you might get one of your own dares." A mischievous grin. "Don't dare me to do anything that you aren't willing to do yourself."

I wasn't one for playing games, so I didn't really know what *dares* to write. I just put down whatever came to mind. Laiken worked furiously, biting her lip as she scribbled on her cards.

When we both finished, she took my cards and flipped through them.

"*Do ten push ups?*" she read with a questioning look. She flipped over the next one. "*Do five pull-ups? Twenty jumping jacks? Ten burpees!?* Bull, this is a game, not a workout."

I shrugged. She rolled her eyes and shuffled my cards up with her own.

Once everything was to her liking, she instructed me to roll my dice. Laiken won the round. She pushed the stack of dares towards me with a gleeful smile, and I pulled the top one off.

On it were the words *Let the other contestant give you a tattoo* in what was obviously Laiken's handwriting.

"You can't give me a tattoo," I said.

Laiken's eyes lit up. "Oh, yes, I can. It'll be temporary." She waved a neon green marker at me. "But it'll be a tattoo, all right." She held out her hand, curling her fingers impatiently. "Give me your arm."

"I don't think so."

"It's part of the *game*," Laiken insisted. "You have to!"

"I don't remember ever agreeing to actually play the game."

"You sat down with me. You wrote dares on the cards. You rolled your dice and lost the round." She ticked the items off on her fingers. "Sounds an awful lot like you're playing the game. Now hand over your arm."

And so, with a long-suffering sigh, I extended my arm towards Laiken.

"Done," she announced fifteen minutes later.

I almost couldn't bring myself to look at my forearm, which now supported an intricate design consisting of Laiken's name surrounded by vivid flowers and swirls. Laiken was a talented artist, I had to admit, but that didn't mean I wanted her art staining my skin.

I glared at Laiken's ever-brightening grin. "Your turn to

pick a dare."

"Oh, no. See, now it's time for round two, and whoever loses will get to do a dare." A wicked grin. "Which just might be you again."

Indeed, I ended up losing the next round and drew my own dare to do ten pushups, which was a piece of cake. Laiken lost the third round, and when she drew her card, she let out a cry of indignation.

"This was meant for you," she pouted, flipping it around so I could read it: *Dye your hair blue.*

I smirked at her. "Draw another, since it's pointless for you to do that one."

"It was pointless for you to do those pushups," she muttered, but she did as I asked and did twenty jumping jacks as punishment.

We played Dare well into the night. While my dares consisted mostly of workouts, Laiken's were plenty creative, which she claimed was a result of spending hours playing the game with her sister. My least favorite of all the dares was *Make up a dance*, which I was horrible at.

Very, very horrible at, according to Laiken. At least, that's what I think she said—she was laughing too hard for me to hear properly.

I couldn't remember the last time I had so much fun. If I ever had. Laiken's laughter was bright and merry, full of joy and delight. It made me smile, and after the utter failure that was my attempt at dancing, I'd burst out laughing as well, which had caused Laiken to give me a funny look and comment on how she didn't think I was capable of laughter.

The banter, the laughter, the silly game… It felt nice. It was the best I'd ever felt since my exile, since my imprisonment—the best I'd felt in years, in fact.

It made me wonder if I even wanted to go back.

Hours later, we were down to the last two cards in the deck, right as Laiken lost the round of dice.

She flipped over the second-to-last card. "Damn it, another one meant for you. *Measure to see how tall you are.*"

I blinked. "Why do you want to know how tall I am?"

"Because I'm curious," she said simply, hunting for a tape measure.

I waited until she returned with it before saying, "I'll take this dare if you promise to do the next one."

Her eyes gleamed. "Deal."

She ordered me to stand against the wall while she grabbed a chair and marked my height with a pencil. Then she had me measure the distance between the line and the ground.

"Six feet, nine and a half inches," she said, letting out a low whistle as she let the tape zip back into its metal container. "You couldn't have made it to seven feet?" She clicked her tongue. "Slacker."

I hadn't actually known how tall I was—I'd never bothered to check—so the number pleased me. "Your turn," I said, nudging her towards the final card. Since it was the last card and we already agreed that Laiken would take it, we didn't bother with the dice. We'd already drawn all of my dares, so it had to be one of Laiken's cards. Which meant she already knew what it was. It couldn't be something bad, otherwise she wouldn't have taken my deal.

She barely glanced at it before showing it to me.

I choked.

Kiss the other contestant.

She blinked innocently at me as I glared. "It's what the game says," she crooned. "Unless you'd rather have the dare."

I hissed. "Does it matter?"

"My thoughts exactly."

Scowling, I reclaimed my seat on the floor. Laiken sauntered over and knelt down so that our eyes were on the same level. Her own eyes were burning with blue fire, sparkling with mischief and wicked delight.

I might hate her after all.

Laiken pressed the card into my hand and whispered, "The dare says so."

And then she kissed me.

I went rigid, every muscle locking up as her lips brushed against mine. Laiken drew back quickly, not quite meeting my gaze.

"Well," she said, and did I imagine how hoarse her voice sounded? Was that disappointment in her expression? She was quick to stand up, to dust off her denim shorts, her gaze never one meeting mine. "The game's over."

"Yeah," I said breathlessly. "It was… fun."

"Yep." She brushed her hair over her shoulder. "It's late. We should get some rest."

Laiken nodded distantly before scooping up the dice and once again disappearing into the back room. I raked a hand through my hair as I stared at her sketchbook, still on the ground where she left it.

What am I doing?

NINETEEN

By some small miracle, the next morning I woke up before Laiken did. She was curled up in her sleeping bag, her hair spilling over her shoulders in a bright river of blue.

My jaw worked as I stood up and padded outside to use the bathroom, careful not to wake her. I could still feel her lips against mine, still see her sapphire eyes boring into mine with that unleashed intensity. What had possessed her to write *Kiss the other contestant* on that piece of paper? What had made her purposefully shuffle the deck of cards so that specific dare was saved for last? I wasn't sure if I wanted to know, even though a small part of me yearned to ask her.

I wanted more of it.

I wanted *her*.

Last night had been an opportunity straight out of heaven. One word, one movement, one arm wrapped around her to keep her close… I could have taken it further.

But I didn't.

And I had no idea why.

I should have kissed her back, at the least. Why hadn't I? I couldn't quite put a finger on it. I hadn't even dared to admit to myself until the sleepless hours of the night that I liked Laiken, that I might want something more with her than the veiled banter we'd exchanged ever since we met.

Slater would lecture me for being this upset over a girl and a kiss, but he didn't know what that girl and that kiss meant to me.

I wasn't even sure of what Laiken meant to me.

I dragged a hand through my hair as I stared at the early morning sky. I caught a glimpse of my arm and cringed. The tattoo Laiken gave me had smeared during sleep, spreading bright swashes of ink over my entire arm. The flowers and letters were now smudged. I soaked a towel in water and tried to scrub it off, but all I managed to achieve was smearing it further.

"*Damn it,*" I muttered.

Scowling, I returned to the main room. Laiken was still asleep underneath one of her handmade stained glass windows. The sun was just beginning to peek through the window, catching on the glittering pieces of glass and sending the bright colors across her sleeping bag and face. I could see why she liked the idea of a stained glass window; there was something magical about it, something simple yet ethereal in its beauty.

I scrubbed my hands over my face. I was letting one kiss get to my head. One stupid, meaningless kiss that happened because of a stupid, meaningless game.

But why did she write that dare to begin with?

Fighting back a sigh, I grabbed my weapons and strapped them on before nudging Laiken awake. "I'm going for a walk," I said.

She barely even cracked open an eye. "Okay," she murmured.

I stood there for a few seconds, unsure of what to do, then walked out.

The air was clear as I walked out, not a cloud to be seen, the sky lightening with pastel shades of pink and orange. The town was just as it looked when I first saw it, save for the pile of corpses gathered around one house—the mutants I killed to save Laiken. That seemed like forever ago, but it had only been a couple of weeks. It felt much longer. Time had a weird way of warping when you were in the wastelands. By my rough estimate, I had been in exile for nearly three months, but it felt like years. Decades, even.

The thought caused me to pause. Nearly three months since Slater allowed me to be exiled, nine since I was arrested. It felt so long ago, but my anger was fresh and livid.

Slater raised me since I was eight years old. He wasn't my father in the traditional sense, but I was closer to him than I ever had been to my real dad, who barely looked my way or spoke to me before he died. Slater personally trained me for years. I followed him without question, killing his targets without ever once doubting him or asking why. I *killed* for him, killed enough people that I was ashamed to admit it to people. When I was caught, I took all the blame, letting myself be labeled as a serial killer and thrown into jail, denying all involvement with Slater, holding onto a promise he never kept. I rotted in a prison cell for six months, waiting for the day of my execution to come.

All for him.

There wasn't a damn thing I could do about it now. It wasn't like I could go talk to him about it, go hash it out with him—I couldn't go anywhere near three hundred yards of the Austin Safe Zone without getting shot. Slater had effectively cut me loose and shielded himself from any retribution I might have planned. And I most certainly had revenge on my mind; if I were to ever see the President of the United States again, no amount of self-control would keep me from punching him square in the jaw. I didn't even care what kind of trouble it would get me into. The satisfaction would be worth it.

I stalked off, silently fuming. A rock was in my path, and I kicked it, my steel-toed boot taking the impact and sending it flying into the face of a nearby building. The delightful twinkle of broken glass greeted me. I picked up the next rock and hurled it at the same spot.

If Laiken could see this, she would probably click her tongue and make some snide comment about the serial killer having a temper tantrum.

That thought calmed me down a bit, even if my breathing was still ragged. I let the next rock thump to the ground and continued walking. Back in Austin, I'd always taken out anger through exercise; even while in prison, I'd done as much as I could do within the confines of my cell. Here in the wastelands, that anger was now directed towards the mutants, so I set off in search of the monsters.

It didn't take me long to find one. I remembered upon first entering this town that one house was blocked off, a message warning against mutants inside spray-painted across the door. I busted open the blockade to find one live mutant inside. Four others were sprawled out dead on the floor, their throats torn open. I killed the one and examined the others. Mutants sometimes turned on each other when they were starved of any other food source. They were *technically* still alive; they lived much longer and in worse conditions than humans, but their hearts still beat and starvation could take them out. There were instances where the mutants would eat their own out of a natural instinct to survive. It was gross to see, but I added them to my total kills nonetheless. Nobody but me would know the difference.

I slowly combed through the rest of the town. Some houses I'd been in before; I skipped those and checked the rest. I found three more mutants, bringing my total up to 544.

My travels with Laiken had helped fuel that number.

Once the town was clear, I set my sights on the surrounding woods. I tracked down every mutant I heard and gutted them without mercy. By the time Laiken found me, leaning against a tree to rest, I was covered in blood and guts, the humidity causing sweat to drip down my face and arms.

"You've been busy," she remarked, leaning on a tree opposite me.

I wiped my brow, following her gaze to the corpse of the last mutant I downed. I could just make out the shape of the buildings through the trees; I'd made a full circle through the woods back to the town.

"Do you need something?" I asked.

She tilted her head. "I was just seeing if you were alright."

"I've just been… thinking."

Her lips quirked into a smile. "I know that's very hard for you."

I glared, and she grinned in response.

"Have you eaten yet?" she asked.

"No." I hadn't been hungry, not after what I'd been thinking about this morning. And seeing the insides of twenty-something mutants over the course of the last few hours hadn't improved my appetite, either.

Laiken played with her necklace, zipping the pendant back and forth on its chain. "You should eat, Bull. I don't want to come out here later and find you on the ground having died of starvation."

She was acting like everything was normal. I wondered if she was thinking about the dare last night, if it kept replaying in her mind the way it did mine. "I guess I'll eat," I said with a small shrug.

Laiken pushed off the tree. "Good. I found some dried

beans in the back of the storage room that need to be eaten."

I rolled my eyes as I stood up myself, rising to my full height. "Fine dining, I see."

"Oh, we're eating like royalty today," Laiken agreed. "Beans and rice are all the rage now."

Before I could stop it, my lips twitched into a smile.

And then a gunshot shattered the air.

TWENTY

Pain tore through the flesh of my left arm. I staggered against the tree, drawing my pistol with my good arm out of instinct. I heard a man's voice yelling, and another calling in response. Then footsteps, heading this way.

I grabbed Laiken's arm. "*Run.*"

We tore through the woods as another bullet splintered the bark of the tree Laiken was leaning against only moments before. I pressed a hand against the bullet wound. I could still use my arm, which I took for a good sign, even if lightning bolts of pain radiated from the wound in my bicep all the way to my fingers. Whoever had shot me, they'd been aiming for my chest—and missed.

I put on a burst of speed, all but dragging Laiken behind me. She screamed as a bullet whistled in the air between us. Loud footsteps crashed behind us. At least two people, maybe three, the gunshots loud enough to suggest it was a rifle. I didn't dare to look back.

"*We got to get Nico, Grant! We found them!*" one voice screamed to the other. A man's voice, deep and amused. I did not recognize it; it wasn't Nico or one of the two people who'd been with him. This was someone else.

Someone dangerous.

"*After them,*" the other called.

"Zigzag," I barked at Laiken, shoving her away from me. I

wove through the trees, making myself a harder target. To my left, Laiken was nothing but a blur of blue among the trees.

Blood dripped down my injured arm. I ignored the pain as I leaped over a small ditch and kept running, gritting my teeth.

"Come back," the first guy called to us. "We just want to talk!"

"This way," Laiken hissed, veering away. She knew this area better than I did, so I followed without question. We sprinted through the trees, putting as much distance between us and our attackers as possible. Another bullet hit another tree, sending chunks of bark flying at our faces. I threw up a hand just in time, but Laiken cursed, and I glanced over to see a fresh cut marring her cheek.

I grabbed Laiken's arm again and pulled to the left as another bullet flew past. We kept running, kicking up a storm of dirt and leaves behind us, our attackers close enough behind us that I could hear their labored breathing as they struggled to keep up.

The trees thinned up ahead. We crashed through the undergrowth, finding ourselves at the top of a small slope.

And at the bottom of the slope was a river.

I cursed, wheeling back before my momentum sent me crashing into the water. Laiken was gasping for breath, but not winded enough to resist a sarcastic comment.

"Now would have been an excellent time to know how to swim, huh?" she panted.

I gritted my teeth. We were at a dead end, and there wasn't much time.

So I gripped my pistol and turned towards our attackers just as they appeared at the top of the slope.

I was on them in an instant, releasing a spray of bullets then ducking behind a wide oak tree before they could return fire. There were two of them, one with raven-black hair, the other with brown. Both tall and muscular. Both bearing heavy rifles—weapons they would be forced to ditch in hand-to-hand combat.

The dark-haired one caught a bullet to the gut and fell with a pained cry. His friend lunged.

And I unleashed myself upon him.

I ducked underneath him as he swung the rifle at my head, coming up underneath his arm with a brutal blow to his chin. He stumbled back. I swung my elbow at his face and ripped the rifle out of his hands, throwing it to the ground.

The other staggered to his feet, one hand pressed against his bleeding stomach. I delivered a swift kick right into his abdomen. He screamed in pain, but I was already turning, my pistol cracking across the other guy's jaw. His head whipped to the side, giving me all the distraction I needed to hook a leg around his ankle and send him crashing to the ground.

And then I shot him in the chest.

I pointed my gun at the remaining man. He scrambled back, but it was too late. I shoved him to the ground, my arm screaming in protest, and planted my boot right over his injury, pressing down hard.

"Who are you?" I snarled.

Blood shined on his lips. He raised a feeble hand, reaching for his fallen gun, but I aimed a savage kick at his wrist. He let out another cry of pain and stopped moving.

"Who are you?" I asked again, putting more weight on his injury.

He let out a low moan. "We're the Vipers," he said around a mouthful of blood.

"Nico sent you," I said, not quite a question but demanding an answer all the same.

His lip curled. "He'll find you," he said. "He'll kill you and the girl—"

"Why are you here?" I demanded.

A bloody grin. "We're everywhere. Hunting. Searching. Waiting." His voice was growing weaker by the minute. "You might have gotten us, but they'll be more. There will *always* be more. *The Vipers will kill you, you filthy—*"

The pistol thundered in my hand as I shot him in the head.

Dead silence followed. Even the birds went quiet, as if they, too, were holding their breath, waiting to see what happened next.

I stalked for the second Viper, finding him sprawled out among the undergrowth, his glassy eyes staring up at the sky. I dragged him over beside his companion, keeping an eye out for any more. Nico traveled with three; I wouldn't put it past his other patrols to do the same.

Laiken slowly approached me, her blue eyes stretched wide as she stared at the two corpses. At me. This was the first time she'd seen me kill a human being. I didn't blame her for looking wary.

But all she said was, "These aren't the same ones."

I stared down at them, rage simmering beneath my skin. "I've said before that the Vipers are bigger than just the three we saw before. They had a name for themselves, something meaningful."

She trembled. "How did they know we were here?"

"I don't know."

I leaned down and began sorting through the Vipers' clothes and bags, pulling out anything of use. The first one had an entire atlas on him. I thumbed through it, my breath hitching as I stumbled across the map that outlined this part of the country.

Colored lines tore across the page. One area in particular was circled, lines of different colors extending out from it. The circled part was marked simply with a *V*. The lines were marked with names.

Laiken leaned over my shoulder and traced a red line with *Grant + David* written next to it. "This is our area," she murmured. And one of the Vipers that attacked us had been named Grant. "What the hell does this mean?"

Writing at the top of the map caught my eye. "*Hunting parties*," I read aloud. I studied the map and the lines again. "Each line represents a different group going out to hunt."

"For us?"

"For something. Probably us." One Viper—David, presumably—screamed *we found them* at his companion. Like they'd been looking for us. Combing the area for us. "Nico didn't know where we went, so he sent out everybody to look for us." The realization hit me. "He doesn't know where we are exactly. This was just a lucky shot for this patrol."

If we had stayed in the church the entire time, they might not have found us at all.

Laiken tapped the center circle, the one marked with the *V*. "And how much would you like to bet that this is where their base is?"

"A lot of money," I breathed, staring at it. I studied the other lines, the names they were labeled with. One blue line in particular caught my eye, spearing towards the ocean and labeled *Boss, Travis, Winston + Mike*. I pointed it out to Laiken. "Nico's party went back to the ocean to look for us there. That's where he expects to find us."

"They have a lot of manpower," Laiken murmured.

Indeed. There were about twenty names written between all the lines, each representing one Viper. I'd just taken out two of them. The rest were still out there, searching—searching in the wrong places, but looking all the same. And if this was how many people Nico was comfortable sending out on patrol, then how many were waiting at his base, ready to defend it if necessary?

The Vipers were bigger than I thought.

I handed the atlas to Laiken and continued searching the bodies. I pulled off a lot of weapons, food and matches, a compass and more maps. I shoved everything of use into the backpack one of them carried and slung it over my shoulder.

"What do we do now?" Laiken asked, folding up the atlas and tucking it into her back pocket. "Besides getting you swimming lessons, of course."

My mind was too preoccupied to be annoyed by that. "This was just a lucky guess. A shot in the dark. Nico doesn't know where we are."

She asked quietly, "But what happens when these two don't come back and he sends out a search party for them? They'll find the bodies, the evidence of the fight, and they'll keep searching for us." She shook her head. "Nico has a vendetta now. He's going to keep looking until he finds us."

I took the map back from Laiken and swept my eyes over it once more, locking in on the *V* in the center of the page, written in black ink.

"Not if we find them first," I whispered.

TWENTY-ONE

Laiken's face drained of color. "You want to find their base?"

I nodded.

"And do what, exactly? Kill everyone?" She crossed her arms. "That seems like a good way to get yourself killed. We don't know how many of them there are or what kind of resources they might have—"

"You underestimate my abilities," I cut in.

"You're injured."

I glanced down at my arm. Blood soaked the sleeve of my t-shirt, dripping down to my forearm, obscuring the tattoo Laiken gave me last night. Fighting back a wince, I probed the wound, sending a flash of pain down my arm. "It's not too bad," I assured her. By whatever lucky chance, the bullet missed its mark. This injury would serve as a future reminder to myself to not let my guard down. I'd gotten too wrapped up in my own thoughts and lost awareness of my surroundings. *Never again*, I promised myself. The Vipers had gotten too close one too many times.

"You are bleeding *everywhere*," she said, pulling a bandana out of her pocket. She pressed it against my arm, and it quickly soaked through with blood. "Come on, we need to get you patched up before this gets infected."

I stepped out of her reach. "I've had worse." Much worse, many times. I'd had more serious injuries just during my time in exile and had managed to patch myself up just fine.

But Laiken grabbed my hand. "Ethan," she said, and the use of my real name alone was enough to make me pause. "I am in full support of taking down these no-good Vipers, but we need to recover first, okay? I mean, you just killed two people. Do you not need a minute to… I don't know, to compose yourself or something?"

I met her gaze evenly. "I am perfectly composed."

I'd killed 153 people. Now 155, two more to add to my total. I did not need a minute to *compose* myself.

To her credit, Laiken didn't back down an inch. "We are going back to the church. Now."

My mind, ever the traitor, returned to last night, and I realized I couldn't refuse her. "Okay," I mumbled, and I let her lead me through the woods back to town, leaving the bodies of the two Vipers behind to be devoured by mutants.

Laiken marched me into the church and ordered me to sit down. She produced a first aid kit and flipped it open, pulling out a length of gauze.

"You're going to need to take off that shirt," she said, frowning.

Not only was it in the way of the injury, but it was still soaked with the blood of all the mutants I killed this morning. It needed to go for sanitary purposes—there was a theory that if a mutant's bodily fluids got into a wound, it was as good as being bitten. I peeled the shirt off, wincing at what the movement did to my arm.

"It's not bad," I told Laiken again. "Just a flesh wound."

She poured a bottle of water over it. It stung. I let out a low hiss as she washed out the wound. She took note of my grimace and eased a bit, her movements soft and gentle. I held still as she wrapped the gauze around my arm, much more than was needed, and finished off the bandage with a small knot.

"I'm not an expert," she admitted. "I don't know how to do stitches or anything."

I tightened the bandage a bit. "It's fine." My gaze snagged on the cut on her cheek, the blood already starting to dry. She stiffened as I grabbed another cloth, soaked it in water, and carefully cleaned the blood off her face. The cut wasn't deep. I dug some ointment out of the first aid kit and swiped it across the injury. My hand was just as gentle as hers had been a moment before.

"Thanks," she whispered when I had finished.

"Thanks to you, too," I murmured.

A small smile curled over her lips. "We make a pretty good team, don't we, Bull?"

"Yeah, I guess we do."

Her smile widened. "We should totally do this more often. Beating up bad guys? Heck, yes."

I shook my head in disbelief. "I don't get it."

"Don't get what?"

"You're always so…*happy*," I said.

"I didn't realize there was anything wrong with that."

I shrugged, distinctly aware of how close we were. The shards of glass in the windows caught the sunlight as it came out from behind a cloud. The room instantly filled with a rainbow of colors that played across Laiken's face, across my bare arms and the white bandage around my bicep.

"We're in the apocalypse," I said at last. "There are mutants roaming everywhere, waiting to kill. Nobody in your hometown understood you, so you decided it was better out here with the monsters than in there. Every day, you slaughter them and pray you survive. And right now, we're stuck battling Nico and his Vipers and worrying they're going to try to slaughter us in our sleep. You just witnessed me kill two of them, and not even fifteen minutes later, you're smiling again. I've spent most of my life miserable, and yet, you're perfectly happy." I stared at her in disbelief. "I just don't get it. I don't get *you*."

Laiken looked down, her blue hair falling into her eyes. "I've always been a half-glass-full kind of person, you know? I've tried the other way; being miserable, being sad, being angry. None of it made me feel good. In a world where things have gone to hell, making yourself feel like hell isn't the answer. So I decided to look on the bright side of things." She smiled softly at the glass in the window, raising one hand to catch the bright reflections. "And that's what made me feel good inside, so I stuck with it." Those piercing eyes met mine. "And what about you? You just said you've spent most of your life miserable, but you don't seem to make much of an effort to change that. I've known you for a couple of weeks now, and you've only started smiling and laughing in the past few days. Doesn't it feel better to smile? To be happy? To go through life thanking God for everything you have instead of cursing Him for not giving you what you think you want?"

I wasn't quite sure I was breathing.

"It does feel better," I breathed. "I just—I'm not—" I drew in a shaky breath. "I don't really know," I admitted. "These past few days with you... It's something I've never experienced before. Something I've never had. I've never met someone quite like you."

She tilted her head. "I'm going to assume that's a compliment."

"It is."

Laiken leaned forward, so close that our breath mingled. "Well, Bull, I've never met anyone quite like you, either," she said, a mischievous glint in her eyes. "And that's a compliment as well."

She was close enough for me to make out the smattering of freckles across the bridge of her nose, the different hues of blue that made up her irises. It was close enough for me to make out every detail of her face.

I closed the gap between us and kissed her.

Unlike me, Laiken did not tense up or pull away. She returned the kiss without hesitation, her arms coming up to hug my neck. I pulled her closer, deepening the kiss, wanting more and more and more. Every thought emptied out of my mind except the need for more.

I couldn't breathe, couldn't think. I was drowning in a sea of blue and unable to swim to the surface. But I didn't want to, didn't need to.

Damn Slater and his false promises. Damn the Council and the government and the Safe Zones. I didn't need them.

I needed *this*.

My hand slid up into Laiken's hair, the blue strands silky between my fingers. She pulled back just a hair, her lips still brushing mine. I could feel her smile against my skin.

"Happy now?" she asked, breathless.

"Very," I whispered back.

She drew back a bit more so she could look me in the eye. "The Vipers can wait a little longer, can't they?"

"They won't know anything is amiss for a few days," I agreed. We both still had our arms wrapped around the other, a tangle of limbs and breathless smiles. I didn't bother to smother the grin curling across my lips. "You're right, by the way."

"About what?"

"In a world that's gone to hell, making yourself feel like

hell isn't the answer."

She traced a finger down my jaw, her touch featherlight. "I usually am right about those kinds of things." She winked. "I am the queen of happiness."

"I don't think anyone is competing with you for that title," I said.

Her grin widened, brighter than I'd ever seen it, as dazzling as the multicolored rays of light that poured in from the stained glass windows. She tugged me towards her, our lips meeting again, and I let myself forget about Nico and the Vipers, forget about Slater and my exile and the reevaluation of my case.

I let myself forget about all of that as I gave in to that feeling of drowning and didn't look back.

TWENTY-TWO

We did not speak about the Vipers the rest of the day.

They didn't even cross my mind, for that matter.

It wasn't until we were sitting down to breakfast the next morning that I saw an extra rifle leaned against the pulpit—a gun taken from the dead Vipers—and remembered what had happened the day before.

I sat down the twisted fork I was eating with and said, "We need to talk about the Vipers."

Laiken glanced up sharply, her smile fading for the first time since yesterday. "You mean going to their base."

"Do you think it's a bad idea?"

"I don't know. You probably know more about this kind of thing than I do."

That was true. I angled my head, considering. "If we *were* going to strike, it would be best to do it when there's as few people there as possible. If Nico and the twenty others are out on their little *hunting parties*, then I'm going to assume they have a skeleton crew back at their base of operations. That will make it easier on us."

"What if they have more than just a skeleton crew?" Laiken countered. "They could have a hundred people, for all we know."

"It will still be easier if there's twenty less people there. If their boss isn't there. Without someone in charge, people are more likely to fall into chaos—and when you're attacking someone, chaos on the opposing side causes panic and disorganization, which can work in your favor."

She bit her lip, considering. I didn't get much sleep last night—after the attack, I had felt it was necessary to keep watch in case there were more Vipers lurking about, so Laiken had curled up against me while I kept watch by the door. Despite all that, I felt alert. Wide-awake. Content, even. It was a good feeling.

Laiken twirled a lock of her hair around her finger. "What would we even want to do with their base? Let's assume a best-case scenario: We get there and find an enormous base with absolutely nobody guarding it. What do we do?"

"Raid it," I said automatically. "Take what we need, destroy everything else. I'm hoping that there are at least a few guards there so they can take a message to Nico about what we did." My jaw clenched. "They've tried to send us a message before. Now it's our turn to send one."

"And you really think that would work?"

"I think the loss of resources will set them back enough that they won't have any choice but to leave us alone."

"Well, now let's assume a worst-case scenario." Laiken tucked her hair behind her ear and leaned forward. "If we get there and there's a bunch of people—"

"Then we backtrack and think up another plan. A way to draw them out and then attack."

"And what if we attack, but they still realize that the two people they sent out didn't come back, so they send out a search party to this area? Or Nico just tracks us here using our footprints?"

"We'll relocate," I said, the answer coming instantly. I gestured around to the church, to the shelves of trinkets.

"You've been here for two years already. Surely you're ready for a change of scenery?"

She frowned. "I guess."

I waved a hand around. "We don't even have to stay in Texas. We can go all the way across the country and find any place we want, just so long as we get away from the Vipers."

"There are other groups," she pointed out.

Which was true—I'd spent plenty of days tracking down such groups and then killing them off one by one. I winced at the memory. "Well, we don't have to go that far, I guess."

Laiken hugged one knee to her chest. "As I said, I'm all for trying to get a point across to the Vipers. I just want to make sure that we don't bring even more trouble on ourselves."

"We should at least go and check out their base," I said. "See what's there, how many people they have, what kind of resources they have access to. After we figure all that out, then we can make a plan."

"That sounds reasonable," she said, stretching her arms overhead. "If that's the case, we'd better get moving."

The prospect of packing up once again and walking for miles and miles did not sit well with me, but since we didn't have any other method of transportation, it's what we were stuck with. I grimaced as I packed up my stuff and laced up my boots. I cringed even harder when I exited the church and realized how hot it was outside, a Texas summer at its finest.

Laiken locked the back door and stowed the key away under a nearby rock. "It's secure," she said, giving the chain a light tug to make sure.

I pulled the atlas out of my pack and studied it. We planned to take the same route the Vipers took on their way here; it was pretty straightforward, cutting from this town to their territory in an almost perfectly straight line. I passed off the map to

Laiken, who took one look at it before pointing in the right direction.

"Adventure awaits," she announced solemnly.

Yet neither of us moved.

I drew in a deep breath. "About yesterday…"

Laiken cut me off with a wave of her hand. "I'm happy if you're happy." She paused. "Actually, I'll probably be happy either way because that's just how I roll, but you get the sentiment."

I rolled my eyes, then bit my lip. "I'm good," I admitted, a bit reluctantly.

"Good. Now get down here so I can kiss you."

I obliged, rolling my eyes once again as I stopped down low enough for her to plant a kiss against my cheek. And then she was marching off, the map tucked under one arm, a bounce in her step that hadn't been there a moment ago.

I shook my head as I trailed after her.

The Vipers' base was a sprawling building in the heart of a grassy field. A paved road disappeared into the trees, leading to the highway a little ways away. Once, the building had been grand, some kind of event hall, beautiful to the last detail. But now, the roof sagged and the walls were faded. The windows bore cracks. Weeds choked the life out of the garden in the back. Spray paint covered the outer walls, most of it stylistic pictures of the letter V or a crude outline of a snake.

It would have easily passed as an abandoned building if not for the two people standing guard, one in the front and one in the back, both of them taking refuge in the shade cast by the building or the nearby trees.

"Looks inviting," Laiken muttered, suppressing a shiver.

I grunted in agreement. It was late morning—the base was about a full day's walk from Laiken's church. We would have gotten here yesterday evening if we'd left earlier in the day.

"Well?" Laiken asked. "What's the plan, big guy?"

We took refuge in a line of trees on the far side of the field, hiding among the undergrowth. I pulled back as one guard turned in our general direction. Laiken and I weren't masters at hiding; with my size and her bright blue hair, concealment wasn't our top skill. We couldn't just stay out here and watch forever. It was a miracle we hadn't been spotted as it was.

I tapped my fingers on a tree root as I studied the building. "We need to get closer," I said at last.

"But how?"

"I'm working on that part."

The sunlight filtered through the trees, dappling the ground. Laiken's eyes looked positively electric in the light as she turned her gaze to me. "We need a distraction to pull one guard away long enough for one of us to get inside." She gestured to the building. "It looks dead in there. I think you were right about there being nobody there."

I scanned the trees opposite us on the other side of the base. "You will be better at distraction. You can hide your hair easier than I can hide my height." Because those two things were our most obvious features.

Laiken grinned. "It's a good thing I have the perfect disguise."

"Disguise?" I asked, but she was already digging through her bag, pulling out...

I snorted as Laiken produced a cowboy hat and dropped it on her head with a flourish.

"I keep this on me for when it's hot and I want the sun out of my eyes, but I always forget I have it." She knotted her hair into a bun and hid it underneath the hat, which was wrinkled from being shoved into her backpack for so long. "How does it look?"

I tucked away a loose strand of hair, hiding every trace of blue so she wouldn't be recognized. "It looks good," I said. "I'll go in the back entrance." The overgrown garden would provide better cover for my entrance and exit. "You keep the guard busy as long as possible; I'll only need a minute or two. If you hear gunshots, feign innocence and get out of there."

I went to stand up, but Laiken grabbed my arm and tugged me back down so she could kiss me. "Be careful."

"You don't know who you're talking to."

I circled around through the trees, putting myself on the opposite side of the building. There I waited until Laiken walked out of the treeline for the guard, the cowboy hat shading her face.

The guard reached for his gun, but one sunny smile from Laiken had him relaxing.

I was too far to hear their conversation. The guard's back was turned, so I launched into a quiet run, ducking behind a row of tangled rose bushes before he turned around.

"I'm Abigail," Laiken was saying, giving a fake name just in case Nico had told the others our real ones. I didn't give Laiken enough credit; for all her flamboyance, she was very intelligent. "Former resident of the Houston Safe Zone, exiled by choice because people didn't like me and I didn't care for them, either." I peeked around the bushes just in time to catch her wink. "But we won't have a problem with that, will we, Mr...?"

"The name's Jonathan," the Viper said. "If you're looking

for a place to crash, I'd be happy to show you inside."

"Oh," Laiken stammered. "I don't want to stay long. I'm headed for the ocean, see, and I want to get there sooner than later. It's still early enough in the day and I'd like to get some more walking in before nightfall. Do you know how far the ocean is from here?"

"It's still a couple of days away," Jonathan said. "I've got some friends down there now on a supply run. But you really should come in and rest because this heat will get to you if you don't. I don't want a pretty thing like you to end up with heatstroke."

The guard nudged open the door. Laiken briefly caught my gaze over Jonathan's shoulder, her eyes wide, and I gave her a thumbs-up in response. She smiled at the guard as he turned back to her. This time, I noted the tension in her shoulders as the Viper led her through the door and into the heart of their base.

TWENTY-THREE

The door swung shut behind them. I counted to thirty, then ducked through the door myself. Laiken and the Viper were nowhere to be seen, but I could hear the deep rumble of his voice from further down the hall. I turned in the opposite direction and began my search—Laiken, I hoped, would use this opportunity to get an inside view of the base for herself.

The hallway was as ramshackle as the outside of the building. Graffiti lined the walls, a detailed painting of snakes battling mutants. I grimaced at the grotesque mural as I hurried past.

A large doorway at the end of the hall opened up into some kind of rec room. It was empty now, but a leaning shelf in one corner held board games and decks of cards and even what looked like a puzzle, all of it salvaged from nearby houses, probably. Another hallway greeted me on the other side of the room and I wasted no time in rushing down it. I didn't know how much time I would have. Laiken's primary goal would be to get the hell out of here, and I needed to be out before she was, because that is when the guard would return to his post.

I all but ran through the base, peering through open doors, taking stock of what was here. Voices echoed from further down the hall, so I threw myself into the nearest room, wincing as the door creaked shut. My breath hitched as the voices continued, their accompanying footsteps growing louder—

then stopping.

Two Vipers were holding a conversation right outside of the room.

I cursed internally as I looked around the room for anything that would be of use. A narrow window revealed what once had been an office but was now a storage room. My mouth dried out as I took it all in.

Weapons. The desk sagged under the weight of a dozen guns. Boxes upon boxes of ammunition were piled underneath it. A crate next to it brimmed with knives of all sizes and makes, ranging from pocket knives to hunting blades to several machetes.

So many weapons—and this is just what the Vipers had in storage.

The two Vipers outside the door continued their conversation. I tuned them out as I crossed the room on silent feet and sorted through the arranged weapons. I'd left my rifle back at our campsite, fearing its bulky weight would hinder any chance at stealth, but now I grabbed a slim gun off the table and found the matching ammunition. There was a duffle bag underneath the desk chocked full of bullets. I quickly went through them, stuffing it full of ammo to fit the guns I owned and pulling out the rest. I stood up with my haul, but my eye caught the crate of knives. I made quick work of sifting through the blades and finding myself another hunting knife almost identical to the one currently strapped to my belt. A knife with a blue hilt caught my attention, and I added it to the bag, knowing Laiken would like it.

I set the strap of the bag on my shoulder and rose to my feet, gripping my new rifle in my hands. If the Vipers came into this room, there was nowhere to go, nowhere to hide except for behind the desk—a place I wasn't even sure I could fit into. Laiken might have been able to squeeze through the window to escape, but it was much too narrow for me. Not for the first time in my life, I found myself cursing my size and my height.

A sudden silence had me freezing in my tracks. A tremor of relief rippled down my spine as I listened to two sets of footsteps fading away, one in either direction. I waited another thirty seconds before daring to ease open the door again, sighing as I saw the hallway was clear.

I needed to get out of here—and fast. I'd been here too long already, the minutes dragged out by the presence of the Vipers forcing me to hide. My time was running short—and so was Laiken's. If her hat came off and the Vipers saw her hair…

I didn't want to think about what would happen. I just had to find her and get out before it did.

The bag of ammo was a heavy weight on my shoulder as I retraced my steps through the base. I winced as I rounded a corner a bit too fast and the bag slammed into my side. I saw the doorway I'd come in and paused long enough to peek through it, to see if the guard had returned to his post. He hadn't, which meant he was still inside, still with Laiken.

I was just closing the door when I heard the shout.

Then the gunshot.

I was sprinting before the shot finished echoing through the hall. I could hear a ruckus up ahead, shouting between the Vipers that I couldn't make out the words of, followed by more gunshots. A Viper popped out of a hallway ahead of me, drawn by the noise. He saw me and opened his mouth to shout.

I barreled him over and kept running.

I was close enough now to make out what some of the Vipers were shouting.

"The girl—"

"Yeah, the blue hair just like the boss said—"

"*Yes*, I'm sure—"

"She went that way—"

The Viper I knocked down regained enough of his senses to scream, "*The giant's here too!*"

The voices ahead of me fell quiet, and I heard footsteps coming in my direction. I shot a glare at the Viper before ducking down the nearest hallway and launching into a full-blown sprint.

The building was a maze of doors and hallways. I was soon lost in its complexity, but I kept running. I could still hear the Vipers, somewhere far behind, but the gunshots had ceased.

Where was Laiken?

I paused, panting lightly. I had to find her. Now. But where had she gone? Was it too much to hope that she'd already found an exit and was hiding out in the woods?

"Laiken?" I hissed, keeping my voice quiet, hoping and praying she would be around here somewhere. But no answer came. Sighing, I cupped my hands around my mouth and shouted her name as loud as I could.

And this time, she answered.

"Bull?" Her voice came from somewhere to my left. I hurtled towards her, wincing as the Vipers renewed their search, attracted to my shout like moths to a flame.

"Where are you?" I shouted. *So much for stealth*, I found myself thinking.

I rounded a corner and nearly slammed into someone— someone with blue hair. I skidded to a stop before I plowed Laiken over. She jumped back, eyes wide. She still had her hat, but her hair had fallen out of its knot, falling to her waist in a tangled mess of blue.

"We have to get out of here," I said.

She didn't complain as I grabbed her by the arm and all but dragged her with me, taking turns at random, scanning the area for a door or window that we could break through. We were deep inside the base now, lost in the maze. And that put us at a disadvantage, because the Vipers no doubt knew this building like the back of their hand.

"I saw at least three different people," Laiken said breathlessly. She could barely keep up with me, but she tried. "Nico isn't here."

Three people, plus the two Vipers I heard talking—I was assuming the one I knocked down was the same one I heard talking—and the guard out front... That meant at least five people here, plus the twenty or so Nico had out looking for us. And that was just the people we knew about.

I swallowed. The Vipers formed a small army.

"Door!" Laiken said suddenly.

There was a metal door with an ancient exit sign hanging crookedly overhead. I let go of Laiken and tried to push it open, panic setting in as I realized it wouldn't budge.

"Is it locked?" she asked.

"I don't know," I grunted, slamming a shoulder against it. The door didn't move. "*Shit.*"

I threw all of my weight into the next blow, but all I succeeded in doing was causing the door to rattle in its frame. There wasn't a lock or blockage that I could see, but it could have been chained up or blocked off from the outside. I rammed my shoulder into it a third time. Then I backed up, cursing, rubbing my sore shoulder.

"Trapped, are we?"

I whirled around to see four Vipers staring us down, guns in hand. One stepped forward, a smirk playing across his face.

"Let us go," I snarled. I stepped to the side, trying to block Laiken from view, but she just stepped around me and crossed her arms.

The Viper just smirked again and cocked his gun. "I don't think so."

TWENTY-FOUR

"Let us go," I said again. The lethal edge to my voice would have made a lesser man tremble, but the Viper just continued giving me the same annoying smirk.

"And why should I do that?" He adjusted his grip on his gun. "You two broke into our headquarters and have caused quite the havoc." His eyes dipped to the duffle bag slung over my shoulder. "And it seems we can add robbery to your list of crimes."

"I didn't break in," Laiken said brightly. "Dear Jonathan insisted I should come in to rest up before the next leg of my journey."

The Viper whipped his head towards Jonathan, who was standing to his right. The guard gave him a sheepish look before glaring at Laiken. "You were just a distraction," he accused. "You wanted me to leave my post."

Laiken clicked her tongue. "I'm not the one who invited me in. It's not my fault you're incompetent at your job."

Jonathan glowered at her, but the first Viper cut him off with a wave of his hand.

"I don't care how you got in here," he drawled. "I just care about handing you over to our boss." A faint smile. "I believe you've met him before. His name's Nico. He's a real friendly fellow, as long as you're not on his bad side."

We were most definitely on his bad side. I aimed my rifle at the Vipers, but there was no way I'd be able to shoot all four of them before they returned fire. This close, there was no way they would miss, no way that both Laiken and I would get out of here unscathed.

I gritted my teeth as I sorted through my options.

"Drop the gun," a different Viper growled.

I tightened my finger on the trigger. "No."

It was amazing how such a simple word could make a person so angry. All four Vipers narrowed their eyes at me, assessing the situation as much as I was. I might not be able to get a shot off without consequences, but they were wondering if they had to abide by the same rules—if they could shoot me in the right place so that I wouldn't be able to shoot them back. So Laiken wouldn't be able to shoot them back, either, because one glance confirmed she had drawn her pistol and was holding it with good enough form to suggest she had trained before. The authorities that ran the Safe Zone in Austin mandated that everyone knew how to shoot a gun and hold a knife, soldier or not, and I wondered if Laiken had gone through such training in Houston or if she'd taught herself.

"We don't mean any trouble to *you*," Laiken said. "Your boss has attacked us, what, three times now? Four? He's tracked us and followed us and tried to kill us a bunch of times. We just came to see if he was here so that we can settle our score. But he isn't here, so we'll just mosey on out of here, and my friend here will leave the stuff he took so you have no reason to make any more trouble with us." She raised one hand in surrender. "Alright?"

Jonathan and the other two men looked as if they were genuinely considering her offer, but the ringleader—I assumed he was the one Nico had put in charge while he was away—narrowed his eyes. "I don't think that's fair, sweetheart. A conflict with our boss is a conflict with us."

Laiken rolled her eyes. "Here we go with the *sweetheart* again. You know I don't like that nickname, right? And who said you had to fight Nico's battles for him? You are your own person. It's not like he owns you."

"Well, you don't own me, either. Now drop the guns. Both of you."

I swapped a look with Laiken. I inclined my head, just a little, and her eyes narrowed in response.

"Fine," I said.

All I needed was for them to relax, for them to take their fingers off the triggers of their guns. That would give me all the advantage I needed. I deposited my rifle on the ground. Beside me, Laiken did the same with her pistol. When we both stood up, I tugged her towards me. To the Vipers, it looked like a protective move, pulling her to me and away from them.

What they didn't see was how her slender frame now hid the pistol still holstered at my side.

"Now the bag," the lead Viper said. Triumph gleamed in his eyes; he thought he was winning. I let the duffle bag drop to the ground with a metallic *thump*, the ammo and weapons inside clinking against each other.

Laiken stepped closer to me, her back pressing into my chest. I wrapped my left arm around her, drawing her close as the Vipers' shoulders relaxed, as they holstered their guns or loosened the grip on their weapons, as the leader handed over his rifle so that he could reach for the bag of ammunition.

With my right hand, I pulled my pistol free.

The Viper's hand was just touching the strap of the duffle bag when I shot him in the shoulder.

I was moving in an instant, pulling Laiken with me as I continued firing at the Vipers. They scattered, groping for weapons as they ducked for cover. I kept running. Laiken and I darted past the lead Viper, who was on the ground, groaning as he tried to staunch the blood flowing from his shoulder.

One second, Laiken was right next to me.

The next, she was gone.

I twisted to see her on the ground, the Viper's hand curled around her ankle. He tripped her, I realized, and it was enough of a distraction for his comrades to free their weapons and return fire. Swearing, I threw myself behind cover as bullets punched holes in the thin walls.

"*Run!*" Laiken screamed.

Running was the smart thing to do—I could come back later, when the Vipers were unprepared, and ambush them in the dead of night. They wouldn't kill her, not when Nico had a score to settle. If he'd given the order to kill, they would have done it long before now.

But I couldn't. I couldn't run, couldn't leave her here, not with how much she meant to me.

I couldn't leave her.

I ducked into a hallway, my back pressed against the wall. I couldn't see the Vipers, but I could hear them. They couldn't see me, either. My breathing turned sharp, panic setting in and blinding me. I buried my head in my hands. They had Laiken. She was on the ground, defenseless without a weapon, and they were going to kill her—

Get it together, Ellis, I thought, but my racing heart refused to listen.

They had Laiken.

No. I had to get a grip.

But—

"No," I hissed out loud.

Running for it was my smartest course of action. Back as

an assassin, I didn't work on joint missions often, but when I did, Slater always emphasized the importance of saving myself over others. It was each man's job to get himself out alive and unharmed. If I were going to run, I should do it now before the Vipers came any closer.

But I couldn't, not when they still had Laiken.

So I palmed my two hunting knives and waited.

The Vipers had fallen quiet. I kept wholly still, steadying my breathing, willing my body to go rigid so I didn't make a single noise. I'd done something like this a hundred times; I grounded myself in the motions of relaxing the tension in my shoulders, of controlling my breath and settling into that determined mindset.

Silence reigned throughout the building.

"Did he run?" Jonathan asked. They couldn't see very far into the hall, couldn't see if I was waiting just around the corner or if I ran for my life.

I heard several clicks—someone checking the ammo left in their rifle. "I think he's gone," the leader said.

"You assholes," Laiken spat. "I said we didn't mean any trouble."

"Your friend shot us!"

"You had us at gunpoint! What were we supposed to do?"

"Tie her up," he spat.

Laiken hissed. I heard the scuffle of boots, then Jonathan said, his tone weary, "We don't have any rope."

"Then find some!"

"We need to find the giant first," someone else said. I was pleased to hear how panicked he sounded. "He could be back at any time."

The leader sighed. "Right. The giant."

"His name's Ethan," Laiken grumbled.

He ignored her. "You two, go find him. He went that way. You, go get the damn rope so we can tie the girl up." A pause. "I don't trust her."

I had the distinct feeling Laiken was smiling at him.

"Go!" he snapped, and there was a flurry of movement. I drew deeper into the shadows as two of the Vipers—the other two besides Jonathan and the leader—shuffled into the hall, holding their rifles in a death-grip. They didn't see me at first, too focused on what was ahead. They thought I had run, that I was waiting up ahead.

So they didn't see me coming until it was too late.

I kicked off the wall, flying towards the two of them. My knife flashed across the face of the one closest to me. Blood sprayed from his cheek. I knocked the gun from his hand before he could retaliate, then shoved him into his companion. They both went crashing into the wall.

The second Viper tried to raise his gun, but I was faster. I darted to his side and delivered a swift blow to his stomach that had him doubling over. I wrenched his rifle out of his hands and slammed the butt into his temple. He went limp and collapsed.

I lunged at the first Viper again, dropping the rifle. He drew a knife of his own and met me blow for blow. He was a decent fighter, the first I'd encountered in a while. I went for his throat, but he ducked underneath my arm and got a lucky shot to my stomach. I grunted, yielding all of one step before lunging again with renewed vigor.

In one smooth motion, I stabbed him in the shoulder and twisted the blade, then used it as leverage to swing myself around to his backside, pressing my other knife against his throat. He gasped.

The fight lasted less than thirty seconds.

Slowly, I walked out of the hallway, pushing the Viper in front of me. He trembled in my grip. The leader was standing in the middle of the room, gaping. He had Laiken at gunpoint, but his hand shook.

I dug the knife deeper into the Viper's throat, gaining a small whimper of pain. "I'd like to propose a trade," I snarled.

Laiken gaped at me as well from her position on the floor. She didn't even seem to notice the gun pointed at her head. The wound in my stomach throbbed. I felt blood, hot and sticky, seeping into my shirt. I didn't have a free hand to press against it. It felt like it was just a flesh wound, but I thought it would need stitches.

I met the leader's gaze, only to see his face had gone pale. "How?" he whispered.

It was Laiken who answered his question. "I might have forgotten to mention," she drawled, "that my friend here is a super-secret government assassin and convicted serial killer."

Her tone was light and joking, but the last of the color drained from the leader's face, and the Viper I had a grip on went very, very still. The shark-like smile I gave to the leader only supported Laiken's claim.

Let them think I was a crazed killer. Let them think I was going to hunt them down in their sleep and murder them for a thrill. I was silently fuming, furious with myself for allowing us to get caught, for allowing myself to sustain an injury in a fight. Furious at the Vipers for causing this problem to begin with. I was in a particularly nasty mood; it was the kind of mood that tended to bring out the worst in me, the embodiment of the serial killer the world thought I was.

Let them think whatever the hell they pleased. I was done caring.

"Let her go," I said to the leader, "or I will kill your friend.

And then you."

And they did not doubt my claim one bit.

"Fine, fine," the leader stammered. He set his gun on the ground and backed away, his arms raised in surrender. Blood stained his shirt from the bullet wound in his shoulder. One look from me had Laiken shooting to her feet. She winced slightly as she put weight on her right foot—the one the Viper had grabbed to trip her, if I remembered correctly. She grabbed the gun and the bag of weapons I'd stolen and limped to my side. I backed towards the doorway, the captive Viper's feet sliding across the floor as I hauled him with me.

"Tell Nico this is his last warning," I told the two Vipers. "If he continues this, I will come back here and kill every last one of you." My lip curled. "And don't you dare doubt for even a second that I won't."

And with that, I shoved the Viper to the floor, wrenching free the knife buried in his shoulder. He hit the ground with a grunt. I sheathed both of my knives and swept one last cool look over the two men before backing out the door, Laiken at my side.

The moment they were out of view, I whipped around, grabbing Laiken's arm and pulling her along with me. Her jaw was set. Neither of us looked back. We didn't talk or even look at each other as we stalked through the halls. We still didn't know where we were.

A door opened ahead of us. I paused as Jonathan stepped out, a length of rope in his hand. The rope he'd been sent to fetch so he could tie Laiken up with it. He froze upon seeing the two of us—me with blood turning my shirt crimson, Laiken with a pistol gripped in her palm. Then he looked past the two of us, noticing the lack of his comrades.

I watched as his face went just as pale as the leader's had.

"Th—The exit is that way," he stammered, pointing down the hall. "T—Take the first left and go down the hall until you f—find the door."

Laiken gave him a small smile to say thank-you. I just shot him a glare before heading in the direction he indicated.

The exit was right where he said it would be. I shoved it open with my shoulder—still aching from where I'd tried to break down the other door—and stormed out, never once looking back to see if I'd been followed.

They wouldn't dare follow me now.

TWENTY-FIVE

I was shaking by the time we made it into the woods, out of sight of the base.

"What is in here?" Laiken grunted, setting down the duffle bag. Sweat gleamed on her brow underneath the cowboy hat. "It's *heavy.*"

"I found a storage room with ammo and guns in it," I said. My tone was dry. "I raided it."

I scooped up the bag, wincing at the weight, and continued on.

We made it to last night's campsite without trouble. I dropped the bag and dug through our original supplies, locating a medical kit at the bottom of my pack. There was a sterilized needle and some thread in a case at the bottom. They had been part of the backpack I'd been given upon exile. Slater himself taught me how to sew up a wound, but I wasn't good at it. My stitches were sloppy and uneven, especially when I treated my own wounds, but it would be enough to stop the bleeding.

Laiken gaped as I pulled up the hem of my shirt, cleaned out the wound, and began.

"You're seriously—" She couldn't even finish.

There was a sickening feeling involved with poking a needle through one's flesh and pulling a string through it. I gritted my teeth, fighting against the cringe that threatened to rise to the surface.

"It needs stitches," I grunted. "And you said you didn't know how."

Laiken pursed her lips and remained quiet.

It didn't take me long to stitch up the stab wound. I didn't think it was too deep—it had been a glancing blow, in and out before much damage was done. My hands were slick with my blood when I finished. I cleaned off the needle and my hands with a water bottle before putting the med kit away. Laiken sat down and massaged her ankle.

"Does that hurt?" I asked.

"Not too bad." She wiggled her foot. "I don't think it's sprained or anything."

I pulled the bag of ammunition towards me and began sifting through it. "We need to divide this up," I said to Laiken without looking at her. "Another bag is going to slow us down."

Laiken grabbed her backpack and my bag, and we went about sorting out the ammo and guns evenly between the three packs. She packed hers so full that not all of her stuff would fit inside.

"I can't get this back in," she grunted, trying to stuff her sketchbook into her bag. I plucked it from her hands and deftly tucked it into the front pocket of my pack. It fit, just barely, and we managed to get the rest of the supplies loaded up.

"This is for you," I said stiffly, handing her the knife I'd grabbed.

She examined its blue hilt and declared, "This is perfect," before leaning in to thank me with a kiss. But it was when I didn't kiss her back that she pulled back, her brows drawing together.

"Is something wrong?" she asked.

"No."

"You're angry."

"I'm not angry."

"Oh, please. There's smoke coming out of your ears, Bull."

I glowered at her as I wrenched the zipper of my pack back into place. "I am fine."

"And the sky is green," Laiken retorted. Her tone caught me by surprise—it was almost angry, an unusual sound for her. "Why are you upset? You got us out of there."

Her tone only served to fuel the fire raging inside of me.

"Do you really want to know why I'm upset?" I demanded. "It's because what we did back there was *stupid*. It was reckless and—"

"Breaking into the base?" she asked, confused. "I know it went sideways, but—"

I shook my head. "It's not that. Missions go wrong all the time." I had learned as much while working under Slater. "But when something goes wrong, I need to do the smart thing. And the smartest move back there was to run, not to engage in a stupid fight."

Laiken scooted closer, confusion glimmering in her sapphire eyes. "But you got us out," she said slowly. "I mean, you did it with barely any trouble at all." She touched my arm. "You have nothing to be upset about."

I pulled away. "You don't understand."

Hurt flashed in her eyes. "You're right, I don't. So why don't you explain it to me?"

For whatever reason, I couldn't bring myself to look her in the eye. "What I did back there was the wrong move," I snarled softly. "Wrong in many ways. I should have escaped, come back here to regroup and think up a plan. But instead of doing that, I stayed, because I didn't want to abandon you. I stayed and fought, and I got myself injured in the process. If I hadn't gotten lucky, you could have been shot." My jaw clenched. "I stayed for you, and it almost got us both killed."

Laiken snorted, and I looked up in shock. "This is ridiculous," she said, rolling her eyes. "You're acting like you can't care about someone because you might lose your edge."

My stormy gaze met hers. "It's not about losing my edge. It's about someone I care about being a weakness to me—and I cannot afford to be weak."

"So what are you saying, Ethan?"

"I'm saying," I hissed, "that I cannot have you making me weak."

I would have done better to slap her across the face. Her features turned to stone as an icy mask slipped over her face, hardening her eyes and causing her to press her lips together.

"What you're saying doesn't make any sense," she said, her voice rough. "Caring for someone is not a weakness. Loving someone does not make you lose your edge. It helps you, actually, because it gives you something—*someone*—to fight for." She searched my gaze. "What you did back there wasn't wrong. You are not weak, Ethan."

"I was," I whispered. "But you're right: I'm not weak." I stood up. "Not anymore."

Laiken shot to her feet. "What does that mean?" When I didn't answer, she grabbed my arm and demanded, her voice rising, "Bull! What does that mean?"

"It means I'm leaving." I wrenched my arm free, not liking how her trembling hand caused me to shake, too.

Laiken stumbled back a step. "Leaving?"

My chest heaved. "One rule when I worked for Slater was that I was never supposed to have a girlfriend. I was always so busy that I didn't have to worry about it—I didn't have the time or the patience for a girl. But now I see why he made that rule, why he picked me, even. I was a kid with no family, just cold indifference to the world. I came with no strings attached." My breathing was ragged. "Because having a girl, a family… It's a liability. A weakness. A risk. There's too much that could go wrong where they are concerned, and when it does go wrong, your vision is clouded when it comes to someone you care about." I shook my head. "I can't have that. Not—Not around you. Because I do care about you, Laiken, and it's going to get both of us killed unless I step away."

"No." The word was barely above a whisper. "No, Ethan, you don't care about me, because if you did, you would stay."

"I'm trying to protect you—"

"You're protecting yourself," she snapped. "I know what's wrong with you. You are afraid to be happy. You're afraid to love, to let yourself feel anything for even a split second. You are a *coward*."

"*Laiken*—"

A tear slipped down her cheek. "I've been through this before, back in Houston with Avery. He never loved anyone but himself, but he pretended otherwise. I thought you two were complete opposites; that he pretended to be a nice guy while he was rotten on the inside, and you pretended to be a bad guy while you were nice on the inside. I just thought that you needed help. A nudge in the right direction. You've never been loved, Ethan, and it kills you to express that feeling. There is nothing wrong with caring for someone. It *helps* you. It fills a hole in your heart, in your *soul*, that nothing else can." She was crying in earnest now, and I stepped towards her, but she retreated from me, step after step. "But you're afraid to let it," she whispered, "and while that won't kill you, it sure as hell will make your life miserable."

"I am trying to do the right thing," I breathed. "You could have *died* in there."

"But I didn't," she whispered. "Because *you* saved me."

"None of this would have ever happened if I hadn't ticked off Nico in the first place."

"You stopped him from robbing me."

I snarled. "Yeah, I was protecting you back then, because for whatever twisted reason, *I cared for you.*" I gestured around. "And look at where it has gotten us! How many times have we had to fight off the Vipers? How many times could we have died? Two days ago, when we were shot at in the woods? If I hadn't been distracted because you kissed me the night before, I would have noticed the Vipers were there, and I would have taken them out *before* they drew blood on the both of us."

Laiken raised a hand to the cut on her cheek, slick with tears. "So what are you going to do?" she demanded. "Just walk off and leave me behind? You're just going to go your separate way and forget I ever existed?"

I hefted my bag over my shoulder. "We'll both move on."

"That's a lie." Her laugh lacked its usual humor, and the bitter sound sent a chill down my spine. "Do you want to know the reason I stayed with you? Why I came back to find you after you told me to go to hell? Because you looked *lost.* Yes, I was lonely, but I'd come to terms with the fact that I'd probably be on my own for a while. I was content for the time being. But then I saw you, tired and dead-eyed and half-starved, and I saw someone that I could help. Someone that I could be a friend to because the Lord knew we both needed it." Her jaw clenched. "It took forever to get you to come out of your shell. And when you finally did, I was so happy, but now you're going backwards. If you keep on this path, you will never know what it is like to have a life with love in it. You will be miserable for the rest of your days." She stepped towards me. "Is that what you want? To be miserable? Is life somehow going to be easier that way?"

I looked down at her.

"I would rather be miserable," I said softly, "than worried about protecting someone every day for the rest of my life."

Laiken stared at me. Her face was red and stained with tears, her hands fisted at her side hard enough to turn her knuckles white. I could see her trembling, either with anger or sadness or fear or some wicked combination of the three. She opened her mouth then closed it again, as if unsure of what to say.

Eventually she shook her head and retreated a step, furiously wiping at her tears. "Fine," she choked out, her voice thick. "If that's the way you feel, then leave."

I hesitated, unsure.

"*Leave!*" she screamed.

I squared my shoulders. "Fine with me."

And with that, I turned on my heel and stalked away.

TWENTY-SIX

It's better this way.

That is what I told myself, what I repeated in my head over and over and over.

It's better this way, it's better this way, it's better this way.

Better to leave after a fight, better to leave while she was angry with me, while I was angry at her. It made the sting of leaving a little less potent, made the blow not quite so brutal. I was trying to protect her because my feelings would get us both hurt.

I blocked everything out as I went on my way. Sometimes I walked. Sometimes I mustered up enough energy to run. I killed mutants and scratched the total number of kills into the dirt when I paused to rest, only caring when the total rose over six hundred. I killed and killed and killed. Days and nights came and went, but I had only the vaguest sense of their passing.

It was better this way.

That's what I told myself, but it hurt all the same.

TWENTY-SEVEN

Thunder cracked across the sky. This storm wasn't near as bad as the one we were trapped in a while back, but it was enough for me to take shelter in the first house I came across even before the first raindrops hit the ground early that evening.

I shoved out the memory. Even thinking about her name hurt.

A chill had settled deep into my stomach and refused to leave, despite the humid heat of the past three or four days. I wasn't even sure how long I'd been walking, how long it had been since I turned my back on *her* and refused to look back. I didn't know why it hurt this much. It shouldn't have hurt. But I pushed all the pain deep, deep down and felt an emptiness in return.

It was better this way.

I took the opportunity to sort through my pack, the first time I'd bothered to do so in a while. I pulled out ammo and gear and arranged them all. My hands stilled as I saw a bulge in the front pocket. I unzipped it and pulled out a familiar purple sketchbook, shoved into the pocket and forgotten.

Her sketchbook.

I stared at the cover. I'd only taken one look at it, on the night we played Dare. It was so tempting to open it up and see what she had drawn.

But anger coiled inside of me, as vicious and poisonous as

a snake.

I hurled the book across the room, nodding in satisfaction as it smacked against the wall, as it fell to the floor half-opened, the pages bending in on each other.

And that's where it stayed when I left the next morning.

The rain was gone, leaving only puddles to remember it by. The air was humid and thick—it felt like walking through hot sludge. I bowed my head and trudged on.

A herd of mutants wandered across my path after only a couple of hours. Cursing, I ducked behind the nearest tree and drew one knife, silently counting the monsters. It was a large herd, too many for me to handle without using a gun, which would draw more.

The bark of the tree was rough against my hand as I gripped it, surveying my options. The roaring flame of anger had extinguished overnight, leaving me with the sad emptiness once again. I was hollow, but resigned.

My total number of kills was 665. One away from the devil's number.

I looked at the herd of mutants.

And then I drew my pistol.

Three mutants were dead before the others registered the noise and turned in my direction. I emptied the pistol, then cocked my rifle and fired it dry. When all of its bullets were gone, I cast it aside and drew both of my knives.

With every slash of my blades, mutants fell. I left a trail of corpses in my wake as I cut my way through the remnants of the herd.

You're just going to go your separate way and forget I ever existed?

Her voice echoed through my head, unbidden. Blood sprayed as I let out a yell and sent another mutant tumbling to the ground.

You've never been loved, Ethan, and it kills you to express that feeling. There is nothing wrong with caring for someone. It helps you. It fills a hole in your heart, in your soul, that nothing else can.

Another mutant lunged. My knife slashed across its throat, but I was already turning away, going for the next kill.

But you're afraid to let it, and while that won't kill you, it sure as hell will make your life miserable.

The battle sang to me, thrumming through my veins, and I felt myself slipping into the same grim determination I'd lived under as Slater's assassin, as the exiled killer.

She had been the one to make it disappear. To draw me out of that cold shell.

Is that what you want? To be miserable? Is life somehow going to be easier that way?

I pulled my knife out of a mutant's chest and whirled, ready for the next one. But they were all dead, sprawled out on the grass, their blood seeping into the dirt.

My blades tumbled from my hands.

"No," I whispered.

I didn't want to be miserable, to fall back into that hollow void.

That's not what I wanted.

I looked over my shoulder, back the way I came.

Then I wiped my bloody knives off on the grass and took off running.

It took me the rest of the morning to retrace my steps, to find the place I'd sheltered in last night. The sketchbook was right where I left it. I scooped it up with trembling fingers.

The first picture was one of a delicate flower. The next showed a sunrise. After that came some rudimentary sketches—I recognized them as the designs for the stained glass windows in the church. I flipped through the rest of the book. The ocean. A cross. Trees. The church. A playground. A drawing of two blonde-haired girls—Laiken before she dyed her hair and what appeared to be her sister. There were even sketches of a familiar person with blonde hair and hazel eyes. Me. Always smiling, never scowling.

It was vivid. Bright. *Happy.* Not one trace of pain or grief or sadness to be found.

I gripped the book and realized there were flecks of mud and blood covering my hands, my face and neck and chest. I'd killed all of those mutants—I was drenched in blood. I hadn't even bothered to count the corpses to know where my total was.

You will be miserable for the rest of your days.

I lived under Slater for most of my life, ever since I was eight years old. All those years, all those hours of training, all those tasks and assignments and missions. He told me once there was honor in my job. I should be proud of it. But I'd been miserable, my feelings buried under a layer of cold indifference.

Before Slater had been my parents, who never gave me more than a few seconds' worth of their attention. They never treated me with love. Then came Slater, who pretended to be a father figure, but he treated me like a weapon to be forged.

Slater, who had broken the most important promise he'd ever given me. Even after all this time, I'd found myself hoping that he could change the Council's mind, that he would come to rescue me from the wastelands.

I squeezed my eyes shut. Laiken was right. I didn't know

how to let myself be happy. But I'd never really tried—not until I met her, and then I'd been too scared to give it a true chance.

I thought of her blue eyes. Her quick smile. Her obscenely bold choice in hair color.

I gingerly closed the sketchbook, righting all the bent pages before placing it back into my bag.

There would be no more waiting on Slater, no more following his stupid rules. Those rules came from a different world, a different mission.

I had my own mission now.

I did not sleep.

Despite the heat, despite my exhaustion, I pressed on for days, resting only when absolutely necessary. I retraced my footsteps through the woods, ignoring the sounds of mutant growls echoing through the trees. I only killed the ones that threatened me—I was done hunting them down.

It was early afternoon when the familiar buildings came into view. I launched into a run, jogging up the street, ignoring the rest of the town, focusing only on the church on the hill. I was assuming Laiken would have gone there after our fight—it had been over a week. If not, she'd return eventually to gather more of her supplies.

And I would be waiting for her.

I slowed as the bell tower came into view. I mounted the hill, but my breath caught in my throat.

The doors to the church were thrown wide open, swaying in the breeze.

I sprinted then, abandoning my pack and palming my weapons. Any semblance of stealth thrown out the window as I burst through the doors, shouting Laiken's name—

I halted in the threshold, chest heaving.

My mind cleared of every thought as I surveyed the damage.

The shelves were overturned, vases shattered and pictures ripped to shreds. The pulpit was nothing more than splinters of wood. Laiken's handcrafted windows had been smashed, the colored shards of glass glittering on the floor. The pews in the corner were destroyed. *Everything* was destroyed. I knew without looking the back rooms were raided and ransacked, stripped of all value.

I gripped my pistol hard enough to turn my knuckles white as my gaze swept across the utter destruction, the ruination of Laiken's sacred space.

Then my gaze snagged on something red. And my lip curled as anger swirled through me, white-hot and begging to be let out.

There was a message painted over the mural behind the baptistry, blood red paint obscuring the scene of the lake and mountains and pine trees.

THE VIPERS WERE HERE.

TWENTY-EIGHT

This time, the paint was dry. It happened a while ago—days ago. The Vipers must have followed Laiken here.

I found her cowboy hat among the wreckage, still wrinkled. It had been discarded on top of the remains of the pulpit. Laiken had most definitely come back here. And somehow, they tracked her. Nico had done that, probably, or someone had just trailed her. It would have been easy to slip after her unnoticed if she was in an emotional state. She came here, and the Vipers followed.

I had left her alone, without protection.

I had failed her.

I shouted Laiken's name, but I knew it was useless. She was long gone—probably taken by the Vipers. I scanned the floor but didn't see any blood. Or a body, for that matter. There weren't even any signs of a fight; the destruction of the church was deliberate, meant to send a message. Laiken might have gone without a fight upon seeing she was outmatched. And they had destroyed her church anyway.

My eyes fell on the cowboy hat once again. I picked it up and dusted it off before dropping it on my own head. The Vipers would not be a problem for much longer.

They had no idea who they were messing with. Who they just pissed off.

Tell Nico this is his last warning.

If he continues this, I will come back here and kill every last one of you.

I checked the number of bullets in my gun and stalked out of the church.

My pack was sitting in the middle of the road, overturned. I scooped it up and flung it over one shoulder. I didn't have the map that showed where the Vipers' base was, but I remembered the way well enough to make it there. Even if I didn't remember the direct route, all I had to do was get close—one of their patrols would find me eventually.

And then they would pay.

I exited the town and stalked through the woods. The sun broke through the clouds and let its golden rays filter through the trees. My gaze fell to the leaves on the ground and I couldn't help but think of Laiken picking one up and twirling it between her fingers as she pondered about God.

It still hurt to think about her, I realized. It sure as hell was not better this way.

I picked up my pace and kept going.

It was tempting to not rest that night, to keep walking so I would be there by morning. But I forced myself to sleep, because I was weary from days of travel and I would need the rest for the fight. In the morning I ate little and instead sharpened my knives. Then I was off again, my long shadow stretching out between the trees.

I arrived at the base by late morning, surprising myself by getting there without the use of a map. It soon became clear that the Vipers were waiting for me. There were no less than three guards outside each entrance, as opposed to the lone Viper from before. Unsurprisingly, I did not see Jonathan among them. He'd abandoned his post to let Laiken inside, then let us go without a fight; it would be a miracle if Nico hadn't ripped him to shreds by now.

The remainder of the day was spent scouting the area. I did not see Nico even once. Or Laiken, for that matter. The Vipers were on high alert—I could see that much from the tension in their shoulders, the way patrols kept glancing behind them and guards kept their finger on the trigger. I marked the faces of each patrol as it went out, making sure every member returned by evening, making sure they were all inside of the base before I began. I didn't want to have to deal with stragglers. The only memorable moment of the day was when a stray cat darted across the field and several Vipers made a game of trying to throw rocks at it. They missed every time, and it was entertaining to see my enemy put down a notch by a scrawny animal.

The sun finally dipped below the horizon. Nightfall came with a hushed silence, as if the birds and crickets and breeze held their breath to see what would happen next.

I glanced up at the sky, where a small sliver of a crescent moon gave the faintest glimmer of light to see by. It was just enough. I checked my pistol, my two newly-sharpened knives. I didn't bring the rifle with me. Stealth would be my biggest weapon. Without it, I didn't stand a chance.

I rose to my feet and slunk through the woods, my tall frame blending into the trees. I circled around to the side of the building. The trio of guards on the backside had flashlights to illuminate the area, but there were plenty of shadows to hide in. The overgrown garden provided more than enough cover— as long as I could get to it without being seen.

The guards mostly stayed in one place, occasionally sweeping their flashlight beams over the treeline. I waited until they were all facing away before launching into a sprint.

I burst out of the trees and flew across the grass, my long strides easily eating up the distance. My feet were near-silent; I'd had plenty of practice at this. One Viper began to swing his flashlight back around to my direction. My breath hitched. I had to make it to the edge of the building, where I would be completely out of sight. There wasn't an entrance back there, but once I was close, I could round the corner and take the guards by surprise.

The light came closer. I gritted my teeth and put on a burst of speed, flinging myself the last few feet. I rolled twice and nearly slammed into the wall, throwing out an arm to stop myself before the crash could alert both sets of guards of my presence.

Flat on my back, I gasped up at the sky. I waited, but nobody came and nobody raised their voice to sound the alarm. Only when I was sure no one had seen or heard me did I pick myself up and dust the grass off my clothes.

It didn't matter to me how long this took. It could take all night for all I cared. I had nothing but time.

I crept to the corner of the building and dared a peek around. The three guards were huddled together. They were scared, I realized, which I wouldn't have minded had it not caused them to exercise extreme caution. Taking on all three of them at once would surely result in a loud, bloody fight, which was something I needed to avoid. I need quick, clean, *quiet* kills. I could do that the easiest in one-on-one encounters.

My eyes scoured the ground under the weak light of the moon. I needed to make a noise, but not a loud one. Just enough to get their attention.

I picked up a rock and weighed it in my hand before gently tossing it back to the ground. The muffled *thump* was enough to bring a pause to the guards' murmured conversation.

"What is that?" one asked, voice low enough I could barely hear it.

"It's probably that cat again," another grumbled. He must have been one to participate in the rock-throwing contest from earlier, then. "I'll go check it out."

The first guard sneered. "I bet you can't hit it with a rock this time, either."

"I can do better than you," he quipped.

One flashlight beam bobbed and grew more intense. I pressed myself against the wall as a Viper rounded the corner, his light held loosely in his hand. He didn't see me until my knife was flashing across his throat, and by then, it was far too late. He made a little choking sound before collapsing. I plucked the flashlight out of his hand before he fell and switched it off.

The other two guards couldn't see what happened around the corner, but they noted the disappearance of the light and the sudden silence and went quiet themselves.

"Nate?" one called, worried. "You good, bro?"

I drew back into the shadows. Blood dripped from my knife to the ground.

There was a soft murmur of conversation between the guards, and then both of their lights switched off. I didn't know what they were trying to accomplish, but I took advantage of the darkness to dart from the corner of the building into the garden, crouching behind a tangle of vines and weeds.

"Do you think it's *him*?" one hissed.

I assumed that meant me—they took Laiken and had since

amped up their guard rotations. They expected me to show up. I didn't move as the second said, "I don't know, dude. The girl said he was gone, didn't she?"

"Josh thinks she's bluffing."

"Does the boss?"

"I dunno."

A few beats of silence.

"What should we do about Nate?" the second asked.

"We should leave him and go back inside."

"After what the boss did to Jonathan? Hell nah."

"But what if he's out here with us? What happened to Nate?"

"He might be playing a prank," he said, but he didn't sound convinced.

I searched the ground for another small rock and tossed it against the side of the building. The resulting clatter had the two guards tensing, the tension in the air thick enough to cut. I waited.

"You should go check it out," the first murmured at long last.

"Me?" he whispered-shouted. "What about you? You're not gonna come with me?"

"One of us has to guard the door."

"Then why don't you let *me* take care of the door, and *you* volunteer to go search for the assassin?"

Word had gotten around, it seemed. I tensed as the first guy let out a sigh and stomped off, finally switching his flashlight back on. The other allowed himself to remain in darkness. I watched as the first stepped around the corner. I saw his body stiffen as he took in the dead Viper's body, but before he could say a word, I jumped the distance between us and grabbed him from behind. With the flashlight pointed in the opposite direction, I was nothing more than a shadow in the night. The Viper tried to yell, but all he got the chance to do was draw in a breath before I slit his throat.

I eased his body to the ground and turned off his flashlight, too.

"What happened?" the remaining guard asked, his voice strung high with terror. Now that he was alone, I wasted no time in stalking around the corner, armed with a flashlight and a knife. By the time he managed to switch on his own light to see who the footsteps belonged to, I was on him.

I dragged the three bodies deeper into the garden. A rudimentary search would uncover them quickly, but I wasn't worried about it. I took a flashlight and switched it on before opening the back door and entering the Vipers' base.

TWENTY-NINE

The hallway was just as I remembered it, though it definitely appeared eerier in the dark. I swept the flashlight back and forth, confirming I was alone. If Nico had put so many guards outside in anticipation of attack, I doubted the rest of the Vipers would be sleeping peacefully in their beds. Nico was smart enough to anticipate a night attack; I figured there would be more guards or patrols roaming the halls of the base itself.

I switched off the flashlight to keep as stealthy as possible and began walking, trailing one hand down the wall to keep myself oriented. I did not know where Nico would be or where the Vipers would keep Laiken, if she was even alive. There was a chance that Nico would have killed her outright. I had no way of knowing the difference, and that thought drove me crazy. If I found out she was dead, Nico was going to get off much, much worse than he was already.

I spotted a light up ahead and quickly ducked to the side. A single Viper strolled down the hall, whistling to himself.

He stopped whistling shortly after.

I left the body on the floor and continued on.

Three more Vipers encountered me in that hallway, and three more Vipers did not survive those encounters. Each one was silent. A knife in the dark, a flashlight turned off, a body eased to the ground. I didn't have to use my pistol. I simply did not need it.

I reached the end of the hall and turned right, slowly making my way around what I thought was the outer layer of the base.

My first real problem was when I came across two Vipers walking together down the hall. A man and a woman, which surprised me—I didn't realize Nico had any women among his ranks. The problem didn't lie in her gender but rather in her very presence; I couldn't take on two people at once without risking one of them shouting for help. I couldn't think of a way to separate them, so I crouched in a doorway and drew my other knife. I waited until they were close before springing on them. For a moment I was afraid my plan wouldn't work, but then I was in front of them, my two knives finding their targets in unison. The two Vipers fell in unison too, and I winced as their bodies thumped to the ground.

My boots were silent against the floor as I stepped over the two of them and kept moving. My eyes had long since adjusted to the dark. I walked on, one hand on the wall to keep me oriented, the other hand extended in front of me to make sure I didn't run face-first into a doorway.

I ignored the doorways on my left and right. If there were Vipers sleeping, I wouldn't seek them out and kill them just for the thrill of it. But the ones I saw standing, actively guarding the base and thus presenting a roadblock between me and Laiken… They went down, efficiently and quietly.

It was almost unfair, how sorely unprepared the Vipers were for me. Even after my message to Nico, my *warning*, and Laiken's claim that I was *a super-secret government assassin and convicted serial killer*, they were still unprepared. They never really stood a chance.

It was almost enough for me to feel sorry for Nico, the leader of this quite remarkable assembly of people and resources.

But he'd brought every bit of this on himself. I'd warned him plenty of times, and he still kept pushing. It was only a matter of time before Nico pushed too far with the wrong person—he just had the horrible luck to do it with me.

The Vipers fell like dominos between my two hunting knives. I cut through them with ease, my blades flashing like quicksilver in the dim light, the weapons no more than extensions of my arms. I trailed through the base and caught them off-guard, caught them while they were alone. I snuck up behind guards and slit their throats or snapped their necks or stabbed them in the chest.

I was wiping off my knives when I heard the shout. The Viper calling the alarm.

"Where's the boss?" a female voice shouted. *"We've got people dead!"*

My head whipped towards the noise. A small curse escaped my lips as another voice shouted in answer, and suddenly the entire base was rampant with chaos. I pushed through the first door I found—a broom closet, of all things—and waited.

Chaos was good for me. I'd been hoping for stealth and silence the entire time, but I would still make this work.

The closet was cramped and uncomfortable. It wasn't long before a lone Viper came jogging up the hall, his breathing ragged and a hatchet gripped in his hand. I waited until he was passing the closet before throwing open the door. It hit him full in the face, breaking his nose with a sickening crunch. He reeled back with a grunt, one hand flying to his face. I stabbed him and threw his body to the ground before retreating back to the closet.

Two other Vipers came soon after and gasped when they saw the body. They ran to it, completely oblivious to the threat at their backs. The backs they left exposed for my blades to sink into.

The shouts seemed to be gathering in a central location deep within the base. I'd bet a lot of money that where the Vipers were now would be where Nico was. My fingers curled around the hilts of my knives as I followed the voices.

I had a feeling someone had given an order to fall back, to meet up together because I was picking them off so easily when they were alone. My suspicions were confirmed when I didn't encounter a single Viper as I walked deeper into the base.

I froze when I saw lights up ahead. Many of them, the drone of panicked voices nearly deafening. I eased closer, using the voices as cover to mask the sound of my footsteps.

There were about a half-dozen Vipers gathered outside a wide pair of double doors. They'd been painted over with the same graffiti the rest of the base bore, but what caught my eye was the blood red spray paint in the center. It spelled out one simple word: *COMMAND*.

Nico's room.

A frown played on my lips as I surveyed the assembled Vipers. There were too many to take on at once for it to be a quiet fight. And so close to the command room, to where Nico undoubtedly waited—because he certainly wasn't among those gathered outside—even the slightest noise could draw his attention.

I quickly turned and retraced my steps, tracking down one of the last men I took down, one with a rifle. I pulled it off the corpse and examined it. I was glad to see it had a full magazine.

The Vipers were still there, still armed to the teeth and wary when I came back. But this time, I abandoned every trace of stealth and opened fire.

Bullets sprayed. Two went down, and one Viper fled outright. The remaining three returned fire, but I was already running. I switched on my flashlight and let my footsteps slap on the ground, making myself an inviting target.

And they took the bait.

I rounded the first corner and slipped back into stealth mode. The flashlight went off and my footsteps quieted once again.

The Vipers didn't slow as they came around a corner. I stuck out a foot and tripped the first one, whose sudden stumble caused the two behind her to crash into her backside, sending all three sprawling. Their position rendered them helpless as I lifted my gun and fired.

I was dripping with blood that was not my own when I returned to the double doors.

There was no sign of the Viper that fled, and I didn't bother chasing him down. I stared at the doors, wondering what was waiting for me on the other side. From my rough estimate, I'd already taken care of the vast majority of Nico's crew. Unless I was sorely mistaken, there weren't many left that could be inside of that room, waiting for me to come and anticipating a fight. I cocked my head to the side, listening, but a hushed silence greeted me, broken only by my own breathing.

Sheathing one knife, I reached for the door handle and was not surprised to find them locked. Whatever waited for me beyond that door, I did not care. I would handle it, because I knew Laiken would be somewhere behind there as well.

Hopefully, she wasn't injured.

Hopefully, she was still alive.

Hopefully, I wasn't too late.

Hopefully, I hadn't failed her completely.

I cocked my pistol and gripped it in one hand, one long knife in the other. A split second later, my boot slammed into the doors. They flew open with enough force to crack and splinter as they boomed open.

My grip tightened as I surveyed the room.

Harsh white lantern-light illuminated the large space, which had once been some kind of formal dining room. A long metal table dominated the space. Standing around the opposite side of the table were two Vipers, ones I recognized: Ren and Josh, the original offenders. Between them stood Nico. His dark eyes were frightening in the white light, shadows twisting his smile into something cruel and wicked.

But what drew my attention was who sat at the head of the table, her wrists tied to the arms of the chair, her face deathly pale as Nico dug his pistol into her temple.

Laiken.

THIRTY

The doors creaked slightly, still clinging onto some of the momentum they gained when I kicked them open. It was the only sound in the room as Nico and I studied each other across the table.

Then Laiken let out something that sounded like a sob, and the sound cracked through me.

Nico inclined his head, the shadows deepening. "Why don't you come sit down?" he invited, his smile sharp. "I believe we have some negotiating to do."

I took one step into the room. Nothing more.

Ren and Josh shuffled on their feet, the former's throat bobbing as he stared at me. I ignored him as I scanned my eyes over Laiken, searching for any obvious injuries. She seemed okay, if a little disheveled. The ropes encircling her wrists were digging in hard enough to leave bruises, though, and I glared at Nico after noting that fact.

"You've been quite busy, haven't you?" Nico asked. His gun did not waver, not one bit, but I kept my gaze firmly on his face. "I've had a lot of reports from my people that they've found their comrades dead on the floor."

"The reporters are dead too," I said softly.

I didn't have to yell the words for both Ren and Josh to flinch. Nico's knuckles whitened as he gripped the pistol tighter.

"I have a proposition," he said. "I'll let the girl go if you turn yourself in."

"Like you would keep your word."

A muscle ticked in his jaw. "You seem to have a tactic you favor for killing my men, don't you? You wait until they are alone before you strike." He gestured to Laiken with his free hand. "I found her alone, and it was the opportune moment. I regret nothing from my previous actions concerning the two of you except that I didn't go about it the right way. All I had to do was find your weakness."

At that word, Laiken's expression shifted, going from terror to something deeper, something sorrowful. Her eyes never left mine. I lifted my gaze to Nico and growled, "She's not a weakness."

Laiken let out another little sob, and it shook me to my core.

But Nico ignored me and continued, "She told us that you had left and weren't coming back. Days passed, and I almost thought she was right. I even lightened up on some of my patrols. Another day or two, and I would have called off the thing entirely and killed the little sweetheart." Laiken shivered as he touched her hair. Anger coursed through me at seeing him touch her like that. Nico withdrew his hand with a small chuckle. "But," he continued, waving a hand in my direction, "here you are. Furious, and rightly so, I suppose. I kidnapped your woman and took your stuff. That's liable to make any man mad, isn't it?"

"The majority of jayour men are dead," I snarled. "If you think you're going to get out of this much better, then think again."

Nico's answering laugh sent a chill down my spine. "Big talk for a big guy. Face the facts, you big oaf: I have the girl at gunpoint, and there is nothing you can do from over there that can stop me from pulling this trigger."

"The person behind you might," I said mildly.

The three Vipers whipped around, guns at the ready.

I let out a laugh at my own and sidled forward a few steps before they turned back around. "I got you," I said to Nico. "Now, what would have happened if I had my gun ready and I shot you in the head right then?" I gestured with my gun. "You underestimate me."

His eyes swept over me, sizing me up. He'd seen me fight, but he had yet to see me *truly* battle against someone, to see me kill someone. He'd only heard stories.

And right now, he was wondering what, exactly, I was truly capable of.

"You have one minute," he breathed. "One minute to decide: Do you want to turn yourself in and let the girl live, or let her die and you walk away free?"

"Lay another hand on her, and I will cut off that hand."

Laiken drew in a sharp breath as Nico dug the gun deeper into her temple. Her blue hair, slick with sweat, stuck to the barrel. My eyes slid to her.

I had a plan.

I made a show of surveying the room, my jaw clenching as I contemplated Nico's offer. But I snuck another glance at Laiken and rocked back on my heels. I had to do it again before understanding dawned in her eyes and she gave me a small nod.

There was only one chance to make this work.

"I surrender," I said to Nico.

Triumph gleamed in his eyes. "Smart move, giant."

I leaned over to set down my weapons, my movements painstakingly slow. The pistol and the knife brushed the ground. My position now gave me a clear view underneath the table. I could see Laiken's legs—also tied to the chair—and the feet of the three Vipers, Nico's behind Laiken's chair.

I readied myself.

And then I screamed, *"Now!"* before launching myself under the table.

Ren and Josh opened fire, but with me out of view underneath the table, its thick metal surface providing a barrier between us, their bullets did not find their target. Nico shouted as Laiken slammed her feet onto the ground, rocking her chair back so it caught him right in the stomach. I saw his feet stumble back, saw the front legs of the chair gain too much air as Laiken rocked too far back and crashed to the floor. Somewhere in the chaos, the lantern hit the ground and shattered, plunging the room into darkness.

It was all the distraction I needed.

I rolled out from underneath the table and pulled the trigger on my pistol, thumbing my flashlight on with my other hand. Ren cried out in pain as I shot him in the leg. He keeled over. I shot at Nico behind him, who scrambled back, blindly firing at me. I turned off the light before he got enough of a visual to locate Laiken.

In the dark, I heard Ren moaning. I followed the sound, knowing Laiken was nearby.

"That was a clever trick," Nico called into the darkness. I paused, listening to his footsteps. It sounded as if he were circling around the opposite side of the table, not trying to find me but trying to line up a good shot. There was no doubt in my mind that if Nico got his way in this fight, there would be no deal, no sparing one of our lives. He wanted both of us dead.

That only made this all the easier.

I kept silent as I inched closer to Ren. Any noise would alert Nico of my location.

"Why don't you talk to me?" Nico taunted. "Don't you want to explain yourself? Don't you want to tell me why it took you so long to rescue your damsel in distress? She seemed *certain* you were out of the picture, and it's hard to fake that kind of emotion. Did you know she was crying when we found her?" He laughed at my sullenness. "Oh, yeah. She was bawling her eyes out."

His voice masked the sound of my breathing as I reached Ren. I blocked out Nico's voice as I lunged, aiming to go past the Viper and to Laiken.

But my hand hit something warm and Ren screamed out, *"He's here! He's here! He's—"*

Idiot. I threw myself to the side, slamming my head on the corner of the massive table, but I drowned out the pain as Nico released a spray of bullets in the direction of the shout. My quick thinking saved me from the bullets that now rained down, the metal table shielding me from the spray, but Ren let out a scream—and then fell very, very quiet.

Nico didn't care about killing his own, as long as he took me out.

Somewhere close to me, Laiken let out a low whimper. I crawled to the sound, my head throbbing. I wondered if I had given myself a concussion.

"Where did you go?" Nico asked. He tried to keep his tone as light and conversational as before, but I felt the darker undertones running beneath it, a sharp and lethal edge to his voice. "Come on, giant, we just want to talk. I have a deal for you."

Two pairs of footsteps shuffled closer as Josh and Nico made their way to me. I felt the edge of an overturned chair and nearly let out a sigh of relief. Laiken felt my hand against her leg and stiffened, but I reached her face in an instant, my hand covering her mouth, my lips against her ear as I murmured the softest of warnings, "*Quiet.*"

The word barely even counted as a whisper. Laiken trembled, but she remained quiet. Trusting me.

There was no way to free her without making a noise and alerting Nico of my position. Once he got close enough, he'd open fire and kill us both. I had to distract him.

I groped along the ground, hissing between my teeth as my hand landed in a pool of something wet and sticky. Ren's blood. I kept feeling around, rewarded at last when I found the knife at Ren's belt. I tested its weight in my hand, then sat up and threw it with every ounce of strength I had.

It must have been a straight shot, sailing straight through the open doors, because I heard it clatter somewhere in the distance. I could only pray it would be enough as I shot to my feet, flicking on the flashlight as I raised my gun.

When the light came on, Nico and Josh were both turned towards the noise. I caught them by surprise, and when they turned to me, the sudden light blinded them.

It was just enough of a distraction to squeeze off three shots before dropping back down.

Someone let out a shout, followed by the distinct sound of a human body thumping to the ground. The person shouted again. It was Nico, I realized, and his voice was filled with enough pain to make me stand up again.

I beamed the flashlight in his direction. Josh was on the ground and his chest wasn't moving. Nico leaned against the wall, gasping for breath, both hands pressed to his stomach and blood dripping between his fingers. His pistol was on the ground by Josh's feet.

He was in so much pain he didn't notice me coming until I grabbed him by the throat and pinned him against the wall. I threw the flashlight on the table, where it spun around, the spinning light making the shadows in the room dance. I pulled out my pistol as Nico choked.

But he stilled as the barrel of my gun, still warm from the shots fired, pressed into his forehead.

THIRTY-ONE

"Are you happy now?" I asked. My tone remained quiet, but there was nothing conversational about it. My fingers curled around his throat, not enough to kill, but enough to suggest that I could if pressured. Nico slumped against the wall, his black eyes stretched wide. "All the times I warned you to stay away from me, all the times that you tried again and again to get me because I made you mad and you thought you could get your revenge." I squeezed harder, and Nico coughed, his fingers clawing at my hand. *"How did it work out for you?"*

The words rang across the room, loud and sharp, enough to make Laiken gasp from where she was still tied up behind me.

But the corners of Nico's lips pulled up into a smile, even as blood gleamed on his teeth.

"You're clever, I'll give you that," he rasped. "A worthy opponent. But I know I'm right about you leaving the girl. I can recognize a genuine feeling when I see one, and the look in her eyes..." He laughed, low and throaty. "You came here out of guilt, didn't you?"

I threw him to the ground, where he landed in a pool of Josh's blood. My boot slammed into his chest. All the air was knocked out of him.

"So what do you plan to do now?" he wheezed. "Kill me? Will it make you feel better for leaving her?"

I knelt down, my knee digging into his chest. His blood soaked through my pants.

"There isn't a thing in this world that would make me feel better for leaving her," I said, my words laced with fury. "*Nothing.*"

Nico's eyes glimmered as he saw an opportunity. "Then it's not too late to stop. You can let me go, and I'll never bother you again, because I know you'll be busy patching things up with her. She's pretty, but you know that already, right? If you hadn't come, I might have been tempted to take her myself." He coughed again, growing weaker by the second. "But I swear it, giant. You let me go, and you will never have to see my face again."

"Just because I said nothing would make me feel better about leaving Laiken doesn't mean killing you won't be extremely satisfying." I angled the gun over his head. "I killed the rest of your men. What made you think I would stop before I got their leader?"

His chest heaved with effort. Even if I didn't pull the trigger, I doubted he would last very long, not with the size of the crimson puddle forming underneath him. Nico was a dead man, and we both knew it.

I saw his throat bob. "Make it quick," he whispered. "I don't want to suffer."

I met his dark gaze.

"You'll suffer enough as it is," I said quietly, then pulled the trigger.

Nico's head snapped back, his eyes going blank as the gunshot finished echoing through the room. I didn't realize how hard I was breathing until it faded, leaving only silence in its place. I stood up and stumbled back. My head throbbed where I'd hit it on the table, and I was fairly sure I'd busted the stitches on my abdomen.

I stared at Nico, at Josh and Ren, at the complete destruction.

And it scared me a little that I didn't feel sorry.

"Ethan?"

I whirled around, my heartbeat racing at the sound of that voice. *Her* voice, so beautiful even when it was shaking. Laiken was still on the ground, her wrists and legs tied to the arm and legs of the chair, her hair spilling on the floor to form a blue halo around her head. Tears spilled down her cheeks.

I couldn't move, not when she was giving me that look. She hated me, and she had every right to—

But then she choked on a sob as she said, "You came back for me."

Those five words were my undoing.

I snapped out of my trance and crossed the room, coming to kneel next to her.

"I'm sorry," I breathed. "I tried to come back, to talk to you, but when I got to the church—"

Her eyes fluttered closed. "They destroyed it," she whispered. "Nico made me watch. He managed to track me—"

"I'm sorry," I said again.

Her eyes opened, and I felt weighed down by the intensity of her sapphire gaze. "It's not your fault they came for me. Not at all. I was angry, so angry with you after you left. Nico's right: I did cry, more than I have in a long time." She sniffed, offering me a weak smile. "I thought you weren't going to come back, and that upset me. What upset me even more is when Nico and his Vipers came into the church and I realized you weren't there to protect me, because *damn*, Bull, it sure is handy having a literal giant following you around. I stayed locked up in the church before you came along because I knew

I couldn't handle myself if I got involved with a dangerous group. You made me feel safe for the first time since I had that falling out with Avery. I felt safe the first moment I saw you, when you saved me from those mutants. And you were annoyed with me, I know. You could barely stand me. But you stayed, and I thought it was a sign."

"I'm sorry," I murmured again, because I didn't know what else to say.

"Did you mean it?" she whispered.

"Mean what?"

"What you said to Nico. That I wasn't a weakness."

My fingers trembled as I reached out a hand to brush Laiken's hair out of her eyes.

"I meant it," I said. "Every word. And I don't care if you *are* something that makes me weak, that takes away my edge. *I don't care*. Because… because…"

Her smile grew a little. "Because I make you happy?"

A laugh bubbled out of me, and I realized my own eyes were wet with unbidden tears. "Yeah," I huffed. "You do make me happy. And I missed you so much this last week. I'm so sorry for leaving you, Laiken."

Laiken smiled at me, not her usual bright grin, but something softer. It made me feel whole.

Then she let out a low laugh and said, "Well, if you really mean that, then you'll cut me loose."

Because she was still tied to the chair. I choked a little as I cleaned off a knife and used it to cut away the ropes. The moment she was free, Laiken sat up and rubbed her bruised wrists. Her gaze flickered to mine.

"I suppose I should say thank you for saving me," she said.

I pressed a kiss against her head. "This shouldn't have happened in the first place. I will burn this world to the ground before I let something happen to you again."

Laiken huffed a laugh, her hand slipping into mine. "I don't doubt you."

I grinned, but it quickly faded. "We should get out of here. I think I got them all, but there might be more hiding out and waiting for the chance to strike."

She nodded distantly, and the two of us stood up—or Laiken tried to, but she swayed on her feet, forcing me to catch her before she collapsed.

"Are you okay?" I demanded.

"I am far from okay," she chided, "but I'm not seriously injured." She winced as she took a step. "Just tired. I haven't slept since they took me. And I also haven't eaten. Have I mentioned that I am very, very hungry?"

"Did they give you water?"

"Yeah, some. But we might as well add dehydration to the list."

Laiken pushed me off of her and used the wall as support to make it to the door. But one step without support and she was rocking on her feet. I caught her again before she could fall. Neither of us deigned to look at the destruction around as, at the three bodies and the bullet holes in the walls.

Sighing, I knelt down on one knee. "Get on." She grinned, opening her mouth to say something. "*Don't*," I growled.

Her eyes sparkled with humor. "You're going to give me a piggyback ride?"

"I'd carry you in my arms, but I need them free." In case there was trouble, I didn't want to have to drop Laiken to reach for my gun. "Just hurry up."

Laiken's smile only widened as she circled around me to clamber onto my back. I stood up, grunting under the extra weight as she locked her arms around my neck and her legs around my waist.

"I hope you do realize how far off the ground I am," she said, peering over my shoulder. "I mean, this is like being up on a stepstool. We are officially in ankle-breaking territory here."

"Duck," was all I said before stooping to get through a doorway. Laiken let out a little yelp as her head almost hit the frame.

I handed her the flashlight, and she shined it over my shoulder as I made my way through the base, trying my best to ignore the occasional body sprawled on the floor. Laiken did not mention them; it would be a conversation for another time, if we ever talked about it at all. I sure wasn't inclined to.

I still wasn't entirely sure of the layout of the building, so it took some time for us to find the exit. We went through the front entrance, and I only remembered at the last second that I hadn't taken out the three guards that were supposed to be out here. But they were gone when we emerged, either called inside and slaughtered, or maybe they fled outright upon hearing the gunshots inside. Either way, they didn't present a problem, so I kept walking, Laiken clinging to me for dear life as she cracked every joke about my height she could come up with.

"You do know why we had an argument to begin with, right?" she asked as I set her down at our campsite. She stretched out her legs as she paused for dramatic effect, a wicked grin playing over her face in the dim morning light. "It's because we couldn't see *eye-to-eye*."

I glared at her. She gave me a cheeky smile, and my stony facade cracked as I allowed myself to give her a small smile in return.

THIRTY-TWO

We sat in silence as the sun cut a path across the sky, its gentle rays warming our faces.

My head throbbed something fierce. Laiken thought I had a concussion and made me spell my name out in the dirt several times to see if my brain was in working order. Beyond Laiken's weakened state from exhaustion and slight starvation, my head seemed to be the worst injury. Laiken scarfed down all the rations left in my pack. I didn't have the stomach to eat, opting instead to clean out the gash on my head and pray it wasn't serious.

At dawn I made myself return to the base. Flies had already begun a crusade against it, and I knew that before long, mutants would be attracted to the smell. I sidestepped the bodies as I searched the building from top to bottom, finally familiarizing myself with the layout as I tracked down our supplies. One thing the Vipers had going for them is that they were well-stocked; they had all kinds of non-perishable food and supplies on top of the stuff they raided from Laiken's church. And they had left nothing behind—I even found Laiken's blue hair dye among their stuff.

I carried as much of it as I could back to our campsite. Laiken wasted no time in using a water bottle to rinse herself off before changing her clothes, which were stained with blood and sweat. I changed as well, glad to peel off my blood-soaked shirt and toss it into the fire.

Exhaustion was dragging at me by that point, so I stretched out on the grass to rest my head. The sun wasn't helping my headache any. I threw a hand over my eyes to block out the light. Grass rustled, and a moment later, something smooth slid into my hand.

I glanced down to see a small glass, then looked up at Laiken, who had another glass and a bottle in her hands. It was the whiskey I'd taken from the house with the skeletons in it.

"I figured you could use a pick-me-up," she said by way of explanation.

I held out my glass. "I thought you didn't like this stuff."

Laiken sat down next to me and poured a healthy amount of the amber-colored liquid into each of our glasses. "Like you said, it's more about the feeling than the taste." She clinked her glass against mine. "Cheers."

I knocked mine back. Laiken drank hers and grimaced.

"So what now?" she asked. She set the whiskey aside and laid back in the grass. Her hair, still damp from where she washed it, fell over her shoulders in a bright river of blue.

"I don't know," I admitted. "I don't really want to go back to the church."

"No, not with what they did to it." She sighed, the sound light and breezy. "My beautiful windows, all destroyed."

"Oh, that reminds me."

Laiken stared at me curiously as I sat up, wincing as my head pounded, and pulled my pack towards me. I dug through it, first pulling out a wrinkled cowboy hat that had Laiken's eyes lighting up. She grinned as I plopped it down on her head.

But she blinked as I pulled something else from my pack.

She drew in a breath as I handed her sketchbook to her.

"I didn't remember I left this with you until the next day," she murmured, thumbing through the pages. I winced at the sight of her bruised wrists. "I figured you would have burned it or something because you were mad."

"I might have thrown it across the room."

She clicked her tongue as she frowned at one of the bent pages. "Naughty."

I watched as she flipped through it. "I looked at it," I said, a bit sheepishly.

"Oh? Was this before or after you chucked it across the room?"

I narrowed my eyes. "After." I bit my lip. "I was going to ask you about one of the pictures. It looked like you and your sister, maybe?"

Laiken must have known exactly which one I meant, because she flipped right to it. "This one? Yeah, that's my sister, Lucy." Her gaze softened as she stared at the picture of the two girls with their matching hair and eyes. Her hand drifted up to play with her necklace, and I realized that her sister must have the other half of the broken heart. "She's the only person I left in Houston that's worth drawing."

"You're blonde," I noted, looking at it over her shoulder.

She pinched me. "Naturally blue hair isn't a thing, you know."

I tilted my head. "Why blue, though? I mean, why dye your hair at all?"

Laiken shrugged as she ran a hand through her waist-long hair. "A few months after I left," she said, "I was looking through some department store. Of course, it was ransacked, but a lot of the beauty products were left behind because they're useless when it comes to survival. That store had all kinds of different dyes. I saw the blue, the picture of the girl on the front, and I wanted to try it." She looked down. "Because it was so bright and bold and there wasn't anyone around to tell me not to." She shrugged again. "I did it once and realized I liked it, so I went back to that store a few weeks later and took their entire inventory of blue hair dye."

I studied her hair. "It is certainly bright."

"I wouldn't have done it otherwise," Laiken said with a grin.

"It's also a waste of water."

"I had running water at the church," she muttered. "Stop complaining about decisions I made before I even met you."

I chuckled as I laid back down. "We could also head back to the ocean, I guess," I said, bringing the conversation back to the topic of where we should go as I slung my arm back over my eyes. "It would have been nice the first time, if not for Nico."

"Nico, the storm, your refusal to learn how to swim…" Laiken ticked them off on her fingers. "It was a *great* time, wasn't it?"

I would have rolled my eyes had the movement not hurt my head. "I'll make a deal with you. If we go back to the ocean, I will let you teach me how to swim."

"Really?" she squealed, excited enough that I frowned at her.

"I'm starting to regret this already," I muttered.

She patted my shoulder. "Oh, you won't regret learning a life-saving skill from the best teacher in the wastelands. We are going to have so much *fun*."

I eyed her warily. "I'm definitely going to regret this."

"And we are definitely heading straight to the ocean," she announced.

"Now?"

"Tomorrow. Or maybe the next day. That's the amazing thing about not having a schedule—we don't have to be anywhere at any particular time."

"Welcome to the wastelands," I intoned.

Laiken smiled as she laid next to me again, her sketchbook clutched to her chest. "You *are* a charmer," she told me. "Heart of gold. Diamond in the rough. The full package."

"I still don't get what that means."

She smacked me on the arm. "It means I like you, dumbass."

I caught her hand and pressed a kiss to her fingers. "I love you, Laiken," I murmured.

Her smile turned softer as she nestled against me, staring up at the canopy of trees overhead, the leaves swaying in the breeze. "I love you too, Bull."

I pulled her close as I matched her smile with one of my own.

TURN THE PAGE FOR
AN EXCLUSIVE
BONUS CHAPTER
FROM
'STARS IN THE SKY'

He wasn't coming back.

The rough bark of the tree dug into my back through my tank top. I fiddled with the cowboy hat in my lap, bending the brim this way and that, staring at the trees in front of me without really seeing them. It had been a full twenty-four hours since Ethan took off through those trees, his long strides eating up the distance, leaving me to listen to his footsteps fade away until nothing but silence remained.

He hadn't even glanced back at me.

The memory had a fresh round of tears rising to the surface. I was glad there wasn't a mirror out here—my face would be red and blotchy, streaked with tears, my blue hair stuck to my sweat-slicked neck in a very unladylike manner. I was a mess, but few things in this world weren't. This was the wastelands, after all. Everything was ravaged and broken.

I stared at the trees Ethan disappeared into and realized with a horrifying amount of certainty that he was not coming back.

Which was fine. I told him to go. Screamed it at him, actually. I'd survived two years in the wastelands after Avery; I could make it a whole lot more without Ethan.

I forced myself to stand up, my legs aching with the movement. It was time to leave; the Viper's base was just on the other side of the tree line. There was no telling when Nico would return, when he would begin his hunt anew. Really, I should have left yesterday, but I'd hung around in hopes that Ethan would cool off and come back.

"Stupid assassin," I muttered.

A low snarl answered me. My heart jumped into my throat as I turned to see a mutant, its bloodshot eyes fixed on me. Cursing under my breath, I palmed a knife and spread my feet apart, shifting into a fighting stance as it lumbered near.

Three stumbling steps brought it to me. I slashed upwards with the knife, grunting as the blade made contact with its neck. Blood sprayed. The mutant gurgled, a horrifying sound if there ever was one, and collapsed at my feet. I shivered as its hands twitched once before falling still.

It was definitely time to go.

I scooped up my fallen bags, grunting at their weight before remembering that we'd shoved them full of the extra ammunition Ethan had nicked from the Viper's base. It was tempting to just leave it all behind—the knife I killed the mutant with was the blue-hilted one he'd chosen specifically for me—but I wasn't stupid. Supplies were supplies. It didn't matter where it came from or who gathered it. I reached into the pocket of my backpack to confirm my sketchbook was there, only to remember at the last second it was stowed away in Ethan's pack.

"Damn it!" I hissed. It wasn't a big deal—I could always find another book. Ethan was no doubt burning the purple sketchbook along with anything else of mine he had. The thought should not have bothered me as much as it did.

Another growl came from the treeline. I backed away, eyes skipping over the campsite to make sure I hadn't left anything else behind. Then I turned on my heel and sprinted away.

The journey back to my church was largely uneventful. A few stray mutants wandered across my path, and I put them down without mercy. I almost found myself wishing for some trouble, for something to happen so I could have a distraction.

Hours dragged by. The night was spent under the shelter of a large oak tree, but I was gone again by morning. Eventually the landscape turned familiar and I found myself walking up the hill to the church. The sight eased something in my chest. It wasn't perfect—birds had made nests in the bell tower, my homemade stained glass windows didn't look as good as the real deal, and it was a far cry from a secure fortress—but it felt like home. It was enough to bring the hint of a smile to my face, a gesture that had been lacking for longer than I liked to admit.

Everything will be fine, I told myself. The world had righted itself after Avery and it would damn well do so again.

I unlocked the back door, letting out a sigh of relief as I entered the building. It was a refuge—that's what it had been long before the Virus ever hit, before there were mutants roaming the land. Churches had been houses of worship, sanctuaries against the evil of the world. At its base, it was just a building, but what it stood for was much more important.

I still believed that, even if nobody else did.

All of my belongings were still in place. The shelves full of trinkets twinkled in the sunlight coming from the colored windows. I tossed my bags aside and ambled down the aisle, my thumbs hooked in the pockets of my denim shorts and the cowboy hat sitting at an angle on my head. These trinkets had been collected over weeks and months. I told Ethan they were a monument to the beauty civilization used to have. My intention was to have this building full of such beauty that if something ever happened to me, someone could walk into this room in a few days or a few years and realize there was more beauty in the world than most people led you to believe. There were vases full of blooming flowers. Paintings on canvases. Windchimes and musical instruments. Little glass figurines. Pictures of happy couples and smiling children.

There was *beauty,* even in a broken world.

My eyes fell on a broken snowglobe, shoved on a shelf in the corner. The water inside was long gone, the glass nothing but a few jagged shards still clinging to one side.

The same snowglobe Ethan had broken the first time he came in here.

You're like a bull in a china shop.

My breathing turned ragged.

I wished I could get over it. Ethan probably had—he was no doubt halfway across the state by now, ambling along without even a second thought, perfectly content now that I wasn't making him *weak.*

His entire argument was stupid. If he wasn't so damn tall, I would have slapped him across the face until he saw reason.

"It's stupid," I said aloud. I glared at the snowglobe. "*You're* stupid!"

I picked it up and hurled it across the room. It thunked against the far wall, the last of the glass falling out. Heat rose inside of me, and I ripped off the hat, trying to find air. I wanted more things to throw, things I could break, something I could rip apart with my bare hands, but I'd worked too hard on everything in the church to destroy it all in a fit of rage.

So I marched outside, picked up the biggest rock I could find, and hurled it through the window of the first house on the street.

The merry twinkling of glass was very calming.

I scooped up another rock and sent it flying through a window on the second floor. My hand was poised to do it again when my gaze snagged on something two houses down. Twenty-something mutant corpses were piled on top of each other in front of a porch on the verge of collapse—the very same porch I'd clambered on top of to get away from the herd when it appeared unexpectedly at the end of the street, blocking me from getting back to the church. Ethan had appeared like a knight in shining armor, if knights wore t-shirts and cowboy boots and packed around AR-15s to kill zombies with.

This entire town had him written all over it. I hadn't even known him that long and he was everywhere. There was the spot where we stood when I spoke to him the first time. As I stormed back to the church, I saw the tree he leaned against while I teased him before the two Vipers had shown up to try and kill us. Back inside was the corner of the church where he slept, the stage where we played Dare, the spot behind the pulpit where we kissed.

I felt like screaming. Ethan had been the one who wanted to leave—it wasn't fair that *I* was the one haunted by him. At least with Avery, escaping to the wastelands meant escaping everything associated with him. The only reminder I had was the scar on my abdomen.

No—I had to stop comparing them. Ethan was nothing like Avery. *Nothing* like him.

A tear dripped down my cheek. I angrily wiped it away as I stormed to the back room, hunting through my supplies until I found a fresh book to draw in. This one was simpler with a plain black cover and thick pages. I yanked my markers out of my pack and plopped down behind the pulpit with every intention to draw my frustrations out on the page.

But my vision went blurry. A wet spot formed on the page of the book, followed by another, and then I was crying in earnest, throwing the book away and hugging my knees to my chest.

It wasn't fair.

It wasn't fair.

It wasn't fair.

And yet I still missed him.

I buried my head between my knees, curling up in a tight ball with my back pressed against the pulpit. My fingers curled around my necklace. The jagged half of the broken heart dug into my thumb as I gripped it tight enough to draw blood.

My sister Lucy had found the matching necklaces while on a supply run in what once was a mall. I'd been sixteen at the time, and Lucy—two years my elder—had just started her assigned work in the Houston Safe Zone. I had waited by the gates after school for her to arrive, growing more worried by the minute. Then she'd shown up with the rest of her group, smiling broadly and bearing a present. After Avery stabbed me, Lucy had been the one to tell me to run away, but she'd made me promise to never take off the necklace. *We'll both keep our necklaces on,* she'd said, fitting the two halves of the heart together, *and every night we can go and look at the same stars and know the other is okay.* You *are going to be okay, Laiken. I know it.*

I hadn't even touched the clasp of the necklace since. And every night, I'd peer up at the stars in the sky, even if it was just for a moment, because it reminded me of all the nights Lucy and I would sit outside and watch constellations glitter in the night as kids. My sister had been the one person who was never annoyed with me, the one who always returned my smile even when I knew she didn't feel like it.

I wished she was here. What I wouldn't give to be able to hug her right now.

Lucy probably thought I was dead.

Another sob racked my body. In the last two years I learned to be okay with being alone. But that didn't stop times like this when I wanted nothing more than to have someone by my side.

We all need a friend.

I thought Ethan was here to stay. That I would have someone for a long time.

But then he left. Called me a risk he couldn't afford and just walked away.

I cried even harder and tried not to think of what a mess I was being right now. But a noise from behind had me freezing, struggling to control my breathing as silent tears flowed down my cheeks. There was a creak of wood, a rush of wind, and what sounded a whole lot like footsteps.

Ethan. He had come back. I was on my feet in an instant, whirling around with a sigh of relief. "Lord a'mercy, Bull, I—"

But it wasn't Ethan who stood in the center of the church, a rifle in his hands and a dozen people standing behind him.

Nico De La Cruz gave me a slow, cruel smile. "Hello, sweetheart."

THE STORY ISN'T OVER!

Check out *Stars in the Sky,* a novella showing Laiken's perspective of the fight with the Vipers. Available now on Amazon.

PLAYLIST

ABOUT THE AUTHOR

JAYDEN THOMPSON first discovered her love of writing at fifteen years old. Her first novel, *Diamond in the Rough*, was published when she was eighteen. A Kentucky native, Jayden spends her time reading, hanging out with family, watching too many YouTube videos, and daydreaming about fictional worlds.

For sneak peeks of upcoming books and more content, you can check out her YouTube channel (@jaydenthompsonauthor), her Instagram (@authorjaydenthompson), and her website (jaydenthompson.com).

SZOA